"What I love about Michelle Ross is her mastery of voice—that wry, thoughtful delivery that opens a door into the stories she shares, that lets the reader peek in through the crack—and her use of language: musical and magical and, ultimately, believable and true. Finally, finally, we have this flash collection that I have been waiting for since I first read the opening story. What I love about Michelle Ross is that her writing exists in this world and I am lucky enough to read it."

—Cathy Ulrich, author of *Ghosts of You*

"Michelle Ross is a magnificent conjurer. She waves her pencil and no one can guess what will arise out of her fictional ether. These stories use science experiments, fables, horror movies, the Girl Scout handbook, and the core elements of what it means to tell a story itself to string themselves tight as a clothesline with tension from end to end. Run and get your copy."

—Sherrie Flick, author of *Thank Your Lucky Stars*

THEY KEPT RUNNING

Previous Winners of the Katherine Anne Porter Prize in Short Fiction

J. Andrew Briseño, series editor
Barbara Rodman, founding editor

The Stuntman's Daughter by Alice Blanchard
Rick DeMarinis, Judge

Here Comes the Roar by Dave Shaw
Marly Swick, Judge

Let's Do by Rebecca Meacham
Jonis Agee, Judge

What Are You Afraid Of? by Michael Hyde
Sharon Oard Warner, Judge

Body Language by Kelly Magee
Dan Chaon, Judge

Wonderful Girl by Aimee La Brie
Bill Roorbach, Judge

Last Known Position by James Mathews
Tom Franklin, Judge

Irish Girl by Tim Johnston
Janet Peery, Judge

A Bright Soothing Noise by Peter Brown
Josip Novakovich, Judge

Out of Time by Geoff Schmidt
Ben Marcus, Judge

Venus in the Afternoon by Tehila Lieberman
Miroslav Penkov, Judge

In These Times the Home Is a Tired Place by Jessica Hollander
Katherine Dunn, Judge

The Year of Perfect Happiness by Becky Adnot-Haynes
Matt Bell, Judge

Last Words of the Holy Ghost by Matt Cashion
Lee K. Abbott, Judge

The Expense of a View by Polly Buckingham
Chris Offutt, Final Judge

ActivAmerica by Meagan Cass
Claire Vaye Watkins, Final Judge

Quantum Convention by Eric Schlich
Dolan Morgan, Final Judge

Orders of Protection by Jenn Hollmeyer
Colin Winnette, Final Judge

Some People Let You Down by Mike Alberti
Zach VandeZande, Final Judge

THEY KEPT RUNNING

Stories by

Michelle Ross

2021 Winner, Katherine Anne Porter Prize in Short Fiction

University of North Texas Press
Denton, Texas

10 9 8 7 6 5 4 3 2 1

Permissions:
University of North Texas Press
1155 Union Circle #311336
Denton, TX 76203-5017

The paper used in this book meets the minimum requirements of the American National Standard for Permanence of Paper for Printed Library Materials, z39.48.1984. Binding materials have been chosen for durability.

Library of Congress Cataloging-in-Publication Data

Names: Ross, Michelle (Michelle N.), author.
Title: They kept running / stories by Michelle Ross.
Other titles: Katherine Anne Porter Prize in Short Fiction series ; no. 20.
Description: Denton, Texas : University of North Texas Press, [2022] |
Series: Number 20 in the Katherine Anne Porter Prize in Short Fiction Series
Identifiers: LCCN 2021052508 (print) | LCCN 2021052509 (ebook) |
ISBN 9781574418637 (paperback) | ISBN 9781574418743 (ebook)
Subjects: LCSH: Women--Arizona--Fiction. | LCGFT: Short stories. | Flash fiction.
Classification: LCC PS3618.O84675 T48 2022 (print) | LCC PS3618.O84675 (ebook) |
DDC 813/.6--dc23/eng/20211103
LC record available at https://lccn.loc.gov/2021052508
LC ebook record available at https://lccn.loc.gov/2021052509

They Kept Running is Number 20 in the Katherine Anne Porter Prize in Short Fiction Series

This is a work of fiction. Any resemblance to actual events or establishments or to persons living or dead is unintentional.

The electronic edition of this book was made possible by the support of the Vick Family Foundation.

CONTENTS

I

Accomplice or Hostage 3
Killer Tomatoes 8
How I Learned About Evolution 14
Men Decide They Want Something 18
Knife Rules 23
Parts We Can Live Without 25
A Treatise on the Broken Heart Idiom 30
Fish Story 33
Lessons 38
Cubist Mother 41
Dendrochronology 42
Bargain 44
Sockets 47
A Girl Scout Is Useful, Thrifty, Cheerful, Courteous, Clean in Thought, and, Above All, Loyal 52
Hostages 54
Hail Satan 59
Before After 62
Why Science Lessons That Involve Potatoes Give Me Grief 65
Dollhouse Furniture 68

II

Phainopepla 71
Fertilizer 75
Three Ways to Eat Quince 76
An Arm or a Palm Frond or a Boot 79
What We Expect to See 81
Feng Shui 86
Glow 96
The Funny Thing 101
The Scream Queen Is Bored 106
Tobe's Baby 110
I'm Just Talking About Water 115
The Point 117
Impulses 120
Before and After 123
Palate Cleanser 125
Eden 127
Binary Code 129

III

One or Two? 135
Business Enough 140
Snapshot 142
Deposition 144
Night Bloom 146
Dead Plant 154

Carrot 158
Snow White with Goats 159
Cake or Pie 162
Frogs in Captivity 165
My Husband Is Always Losing Things 167
Return 171
No Knees 174
Common Denominator 176
High Ground 180
Things My Son Knows 184
Barrel Cactus 188
Tea Kettles 192
Migration 196
Manhandle 200
Muscle Memory 204

Acknowledgments 209

Accomplice or Hostage

In the girl's copy of *Snow White*, an illustration shows the old hag peeling off her own face. Of course, the face is merely a mask that the queen had used to conceal her true face.

The girl first glimpses her mother's second face when they are eating snow cones in the car, the windows rolled down, the girl's skin gritty and sticky. Two other girls, their hair in braids, walk past, and the girl's mother calls out, "Hey there. Want to get in the car and be my little girls?" She cackles. Her eyes are wild, her lips cherry red.

The girls walking by look at the girl in the car as though they're trying to decide whether she's her mother's accomplice or hostage. They pick up their pace.

For as long as the girl can remember, her mother has warned about men who drive around town looking to lure girls into their vehicles. They use lost puppies and Happy Meals as bait. In hotels, these men look out through peep holes, their hands clammy on doorknobs.

The girl's mother has cautioned that the girl must always be vigilant. She must always be ready to run.

In the snow cone stand's parking lot, the girl says, "What if they had gotten into the car?"

Her mother says, "Then you would have had two sisters." She laughs again. "Want another snow cone?"

The girl thinks this new face must be a mask, but what if this is her mother's real face, the other face a mask?

The girl watches her mother carefully during the drive home, observes details she's never noticed before. Like when her mother turns to look over her right shoulder before switching lanes, the skin on her neck creases like the plump, wrinkled segments of a caterpillar. When another driver cuts closely in front of their car, the girl's mother's knuckles become bony snake's eyes.

The girl peers through the cracked bathroom door as her mother pinches and poses before the mirror as though she's rearranging furniture. Her mother talks to herself, repeats phrases over and over, such as "That's right. I did" and "What do you mean 'what do I mean?'"

The girl tiptoes into her mother's bedroom when her mother is napping away some mysterious pain she says she doesn't have the words to describe. The girl opens drawers, fingers a strange black lace garment. The girl's mother shifts in her sleep, and the girl ducks to the floor, her chest a hot, heavy, buzzing thing like the lawnmower the neighbor boy pushes across their yard every Saturday.

*

It has always been just the two of them, the girl's mother says. The girl knows this can't be true, but her mother won't speak of a time before, as though they were born in the same instant, of the same lightning bolt strike, in the same primordial soup.

In the stories the girl's mother tells, girls' lives shift like the colored flecks in a kaleidoscope. They are hunted and abandoned, stolen and traded. Almost always their real mothers are dead, but what happened to those mothers happened before the story begins.

When the girl's mother tells her the story of Hansel and Gretel, she goes on and on about the gingerbread house, as though she's selling real estate. The doorknobs are gum drops. The electrical circuits are strands of licorice. The plumbing is made up of rainbow-colored candy straws.

"And the witch?" the girl says one evening. "Tell me about the witch."

Her mother looks at her curiously. "What do you mean?"

"Tell me who she really is," the girl says. "Where did she come from? What was her childhood like?"

Her mother thinks for a moment and then says, "That story is too terrible for little girls' ears."

"It can't be any more terrible than the stories of Riding Hood and Belle and Snow White," the girl says.

Her mother laughs, says, "Those girls have it easy." She turns out the light.

*

When they see the small child crying on the beach, the girl's mother says to the girl, "Go ask her if she's lost."

The girl says, "Why don't you do it?"

"Because I'm an adult. She's less likely to be scared of you."

"What if she is lost? What can I do about it?" the girl says.

"Bring her to me," the girl's mother says.

The girl doesn't ask what her mother plans to do with the child, but she imagines awful things—the child locked inside a bird cage, tied to a spit and roasted over open flames. Not that she really believes her mother would hurt the child, but, well, she's no longer sure her mother wouldn't.

The girl walks slowly across the wet sand. She says to the child, "Have you lost your mother?"

The child nods.

"What does she look like?" the girl says.

The child seems confused by this. She says, "Like my mommy."

The girl turns toward her mother, who is watching them, her hand shielding her eyes. Her yellow terrycloth dress is worn and wet, and the girl can make out the curve of her mother's breasts, the darkening around her nipples.

When the girl turns back, the child is pointing in the direction of the girl's mother.

"I see her," the child says.

The girl thinks the child is pointing at her own mother. She says, "That's not your mother."

But the child ignores her. She takes off running.

The beach is crowded, frantic—people throwing Frisbees and flying kites and charging into waves. The light is thick, hazy. The girl worries that the child is mistaken, like a toddler wrapping herself around the wrong pair of smooth, bare legs at a party. The girl worries that the child will notice too late that she has run in the wrong direction.

Killer Tomatoes

The man who calls himself Uncle Rick, but who isn't Lindsey's uncle, knocks on the door of the house just as fog fills a darkened doorway on the television screen and the figure of Elvira emerges. Cut to a lightning bolt, then a rickety mansion, and then back to Elvira as she stumble-dances down the dark hallway, her immense cleavage dissolving into a flame. In the next shot, she's lying on that red chaise lounge. She says, *Hello, darling, and welcome to the show.*

Through the crack between the door and its frame, Lindsey says, "Shana isn't here."

The man who calls himself Uncle Rick glows red beneath the porchlight, a novelty Christmas bulb Lindsey's mother has yet to replace (though it's March). He says, "Aren't you going to invite me in?"

Lindsey isn't going to invite him in, but her friend Cheyenne gets up from the couch. Cheyenne's wearing what she calls her Madonna shirt, a white lace tank top that is see-through. She fingers the chain lock as though it's an exposed bra strap. "Who do we have here?"

He says, "You can call me Uncle Rick."

"He's not my uncle," Lindsey says.

What he is: an on-again, off-again hookup of her mother's, a man who has meandered in and out of their lives for years, like a stray cat scratching at their door for a can of tuna when the hunting's slow.

This time around he'd been away a couple of years. Then last Sunday Lindsey woke to find him sitting at the kitchen table while her mother made pancakes from a box. He held up the syrup bottle, his index finger pressed against the glass woman's sexless pillow of a bosom and said, "Shana, what is this shit? It sure as hell isn't maple syrup." When he turned and saw Lindsey, his eyes seemed to stick to her like chewing gum she couldn't remove all the gluey threads of. He said, "I remember when you were no taller than my thighs. Now look at you. You have ten boyfriends?" She pictured herself sawed into ten equal pieces, like a piece of lumber. Her mother said, "She's barely thirteen." He said, "That don't mean a thing."

Now he says, "I didn't say I was *your* uncle."

Cheyenne unhooks the chain. "Your hands steady?" She cocks her hip and wiggles her toes. "Lindsey's paint job looks like a toddler fingerpainting."

He says, "I don't paint toenails." He's looking at Lindsey, not Cheyenne. It's like Jason Kink all over again.

Cheyenne practically handing herself over on a platter, but the boy—in this case, man—licking his lips at Lindsey, who is offering nothing.

Elvira announces the night's film, *Attack of the Killer Tomatoes!* Then she says, "Speaking of grabbers, I have a few choice words for that guy in the supermarket who grabbed me by the tomatoes!"

Cheyenne laughs. So does the man who calls himself Uncle Rick. His gut quakes. It's like the hard mound of earth marking the gravesite of Lindsey's late pet guinea pig, Sweet Dreams Are Made of This.

Lindsey thinks about how delicate tomatoes are. Grab them too roughly, and they rupture. Elvira's breasts look anything but delicate. More like bowling balls: set them loose down a lane, and they'd decimate every pin in their way.

The man who calls himself Uncle Rick turns to Lindsey. "I should call you Licorice Sticks. Those legs of yours go all the way up to your neck."

She pictures an overlay in a science textbook: a transparent plastic sheet printed with the lower half of her body and beneath that, a regular paper page printed with her whole body. The overlay version of her vagina lines up perfectly with her paper mouth. Like some kind of sex monster.

Cheyenne says, "Daddy Long Legs. Like the spider? That's what we call her." She props her toes up on the coffee table, opens the bottle of black polish. "It's not fair she has big boobs when she's so skinny. Skinny girls are supposed to be flat."

The man who calls himself Uncle Rick says, "Says who?"

When Cheyenne introduced Lindsey to Elvira, Lindsey said, "Is she supposed to be some sort of a monster?" Cheyenne said, "What? You mean her monster boobs?" Lindsey said, "That's not what I mean." She'd wondered if Elvira was a vampire. Still, Cheyenne had been right in some way. It isn't just the dress, hair, and make-up that make Elvira seem monstrous.

Lindsey says now, "Stop talking about my body."

Cheyenne snorts.

On the television, a woman washes dishes. A strange gibberish sound issues from the sink. In the drain, a tomato wriggles. The tomato shimmies onto the counter and down to the floor. The woman backs away. She screams. What the tomato does to her, if it does anything, happens off camera. The opening credits begin.

Cheyenne grins, says, "This is going to be hilarious. Is there anything more ridiculous?"

Not so long ago, Lindsey would have agreed that killer tomatoes topped the chart of absurdity. She isn't so sure anymore, though. The idea of this man, who once propped her up on his shoulders at a Mardi Gras parade so she could see the floats, and who is about three times her age, now wanting to stick his dick in her seems every bit as farfetched as a killer tomato. But the way he's looking at her, as though he's considering an extravagant purchase, suggests otherwise.

Or take Jason Kink grabbing her breasts with the casual ease with which he lifts his backpack and lunchbox when the school bus appears. He told her that her own best friend told him Lindsey wanted him to touch her but was too shy to say anything. Lindsey called him a liar. But, later, when Lindsey confronted her, Cheyenne said, "Are you kidding? You should thank me!"

Now Cheyenne says to Lindsey, "Maybe this is just the beginning."

"What?" Lindsey says.

"Your boobs. Maybe they mean you're going to get fat all over. Like you know how when you blow up those long, skinny balloons, the balloons plump up in just one little section at first? But then as you keep blowing, the rest of the balloon catches up?"

The man who calls himself Uncle Rick laughs with his hand on his belly as though to prevent it from experiencing the other fate of balloons.

Lindsey says, "I'm not a balloon." Then she says, "Like I said, Shana isn't here. And I don't know when she's coming back."

"Who says I came by to see your mother?" he says. "How about going for a ride?"

Cheyenne says, "Where to?"

"Where do you want to go?"

Lindsey says, "It's late."

Cheyenne says, "A million miles away."

"A million miles away it is."

Cheyenne jumps up and grabs her purse. "You think the tomatoes are fanged like Dracula? Or that they slash their victims like the killers in *Halloween* and *The Texas Chain Saw Massacre*?"

Lindsey says, "Why don't we stay and find out?"

His hand on the front door, the man who calls himself Uncle Rick says, "Maybe they kill in a way that you can't imagine."

Again, Cheyenne laughs. Like Elvira, Cheyenne laughs at everything, even the scary movies that aren't supposed to be funny.

Lindsey wonders if the man who calls himself Uncle Rick is correct, that her imagination is stunted in this respect. But then he opens the door, and the red glow of the porchlight washes over him again, only this time, the light feels like a cue. Like lightning or cacophonous music in a horror movie. She can't know for certain what will happen, but she is learning to anticipate the unthinkable.

How I Learned About Evolution

Dad wouldn't let me go to school with the other kids in town. He said school was for people who couldn't or wouldn't think for themselves. Other things that were for such people: the internet, greeting cards, and breakfast cereal, to name a few.

Dad worked as an inspector for a sports sock manufacturer. His job was to check socks for imperfections—holes, loose threads, and whatever else went wrong with socks. He had an eye for flaws and took pride in finding more defective socks than any other inspector. Officially, Mom was my teacher. She didn't have a job outside the house, though she did have laundry and dishes and a toilet to scrub. Unofficially, they split the curriculum pretty evenly. Mom taught me rain with a silver metal colander. "See how the water pours out of all those holes?" Dad taught me sun with a yellow flashlight. "It turns on for day. It turns off for night." He flicked the flashlight's chunky switch. Mom taught me Earth with a buttermilk pancake. "We're about right here," she said, pointing just off-center of the middle. Dad taught me birds with a helium balloon. "It's filled with flying gas."

Dad was an inventor when he wasn't inspecting socks or overseeing my education. Perhaps he thought of himself as an artist. He didn't apply a word to his tinkering in the shed with scraps of metal and wood and string. He built countless useless things. Over the years, these things proliferated in our yard and our home, crowding out everything else. Grass yellowed and then crumbled, because sunlight no longer touched it. Trees became stunted, gnarled. I bruised and scraped as I made my way to the bathroom in the dark of night.

Mom never spoke a disparaging word about Dad's creations, but she navigated our house gingerly, as though any step could set off a booby trap. Sometimes I found her staring worriedly at one of his hunks of metal like she had at the trail of ants that entered our house from a crack in the wall above the kitchen sink one dry summer or the lone earwig she'd once found wedged between bristles of her toothbrush. When she saw me, she'd return to her cleaning or cooking or mending. She'd smile, the worried look flicked away like a speck of grit from her eye.

Then one day, Dad erected a thing so enormous, so hulking, I said, "It looks like a dinosaur."

We were out near the shed. It was dusk. He'd been teaching me fireflies. "Like the sun, only smaller, and on and off faster," he said. "They have to blink off frequently or else they'd burn alive."

When I glimpsed the shadowy, towering figure through the shed's darkened doorway, my spine tingled.

Dad's expression quickly sharpened. "Dinosaur? What do you know about dinosaurs?"

I told him Mom had taught me that humans were why the dinosaurs went extinct. We overhunted them.

"Extinct?" he said. "What do you know about extinction?"

When Mom emerged from the bathroom after taking her nightly bath, Dad and I were waiting for her in the hallway. He was squeezing my arm too hard, as though he were trying to crush whatever was inside.

He said, "You believe in dinosaurs?"

Mom's hair was wrapped in a red towel that sat upon her head like a lampshade. She was silent for a long moment. Then she said, "I saw a footprint of one once. In Utah. When I was her age. It was the size of a toddler."

Dad said, "A footprint? You mean a shape carved in dirt?" He shook his head in disgust.

Mom said nothing, but I saw with *my* eyes how her face shifted.

Another lesson I'd learned via pancakes, though this one I'd acquired without either of my parents' instruction, was irreversible change—how some transformations, such as gooey, drippy pancake batter cooking on a hot griddle, can't be undone. When a pancake wrinkles around the edges, a signal that it's cooked on bottom, you better flip that pancake fast before it scorches, before it's ruined. There isn't any starting over. Hardened batter is no longer and never will be batter again.

Men Decide They Want Something

On their walk to see the world's most famous geyser, Anne's father swung his arms in that breezy way of his, as though the world were a shiny package with his name on it. Anne's mother had stayed behind in the motor home Anne's parents had rented for their three-week tour of the national parks of the West. A few days earlier, Anne's mother had missed the redwoods, too. The way she crossed her arms, tight as a constrictor knot, she seemed to Anne like a genie trapped inside a lamp. That made Anne's father the untethered mortal, perfectly content to let the genie remain bottled up.

While they waited for the geyser to erupt, a woman with long, long legs, her shorts like the red tips of two matchsticks, smiled at them. Anne thought of the women in the magazines hidden behind her father's record collection, their legs wishbones. Anne's mother was no wishbone. But sometimes she was a spine, the bone that took grit to cut from a chicken's back if you wanted to butterfly the bird and roast it with potatoes and carrots and butter. Other times she was more like a wing bone, folded in on herself.

Anne's father smiled back, and Anne thought, this is how highways are made to tunnel through mountains: men decide they want something.

Anne had read at the Visitor Center that Old Faithful was once used as a laundromat. The first white men to set foot in Yellowstone—trappers, fur traders, miners, gold prospectors, explorers—didn't have wives in tow to do their washing for them. They laid out their sweat-stained clothing while the geyser was quiet, placid. They backed away and waited for her to erupt.

There was no doubt in Anne's mind that they referred to the geyser as "she."

Anne decided that she would buy her poor mother a gift in the souvenir shop.

She chose a shot glass, thinking it was like the thimbles her grandmother collected, a trinket meant for display. But when she presented it to her mother that evening, her mother said, "I don't mind if I do." Then to Anne's father, "This your idea? Get me so drunk I'll forget?"

He said, "Don't blame me. I told her to save her money."

Anne's mother drank tequila from the little glass etched with a drawing of Old Faithful erupting. Anne imagined the liquor hot and bubbling inside her mother.

Geysers erupt because they have a circulation glitch. Heat gets trapped deep inside. The heat eventually becomes so great that it overwhelms the pressure preventing its release. Like holding one's breath. Most people can fight the impulse to exhale for only thirty seconds or so, maybe a minute if they've practiced. The buildup of carbon dioxide makes the chest feel like it's going to explode.

Anne's record was a minute and twelve seconds.

After several pours of tequila, Anne's mother set up Sorry on the motor home's little dining table.

Anne's father had a habit of moving his pawns before he'd counted. When Anne's mother criticized, he said he didn't need to count because he had the instinct of a Jedi. That evening, however, he landed a pawn on a space occupied by one of his own pawns, an illegal move.

Anne's mother shook her head. To Anne's father, she said, "I'm surprised your Jedi powers didn't guide your hand swiftly to the pawn that can kill my pawn."

To Anne, she said, "Your daddy believes that everything will work out in his favor, that no effort or forethought is required."

Anne thought about how earlier that day, her father had led them off-trail despite signs warning about the contamination of delicate ecosystems and the physical dangers of hot springs. He'd waved his hand in dismissal, said, "They just don't want everybody doing it."

Anne's father said now, "Well, since it's against the rules to land on my own pawn's space, I guess I have to kill you."

Anne's mother said, "No, you don't. It's a choice. Take responsibility for your goddamn actions."

Anne's father sighed. He picked up the only other blue pawn he still had in play, counted ten spaces, and landed on a space occupied by one of Anne's yellow pawns. "Sorry to have to kill you, sweetie."

Anne said, "Sending a pawn back to start doesn't kill it."

Her mother said, "That's one way to see it."

That night when they thought Anne was asleep, her mother said, "I'm maxed out. Full to the brim."

Anne had read that everything from socks to bath towels to a sofa had been found in the Yellowstone geysers and pools. That's why Morning Glory Pool's colors had faded from a shimmering sapphire to a rusted blue.

What else she'd read: A tourist recently wandered off the designated paths and fell into an acidic hot spring. His remains were unrecoverable. Other tourists had been gored by bison, one because he was trying to take a selfie with the animal. A man and his son loaded a baby bison into the back of their SUV because they thought it was cold. The animal had to be euthanized.

Upon exiting the park the next day, Anne's father drove over two squirrels crossing the road. These were the second and third incidences of vehicular squirrel-slaughter during their grand tour of the national parks of the West. The squirrel's bones beneath the tires shook Anne and her parents as though they were pennies in a jar. Anne's mother screamed. Anne's father said nothing, kept driving. The way he gripped the wheel, Anne hoped that nothing else got in his way.

Knife Rules

They don't talk about their becoming knives. We don't talk about their becoming knives. None of us talk about knives at all. When onions must be diced, the dicer chokes the chopping knife handle with her fist. She works quickly but carefully. She washes the blade, puts the knife away.

Kitchen knives are different. They're completely under our control. Still, we don't talk about kitchen knives, either.

We wrap our younger siblings' hands around sleek black handles. Show them how to chop without a word. We show them the first aid supplies, too. How to clean and bandage a wound. How to stitch a gash.

When a finger is severed, we don't talk about the how or the who. We place the finger in a plastic bag, swaddle it in crushed ice. We deliver the finger and its owner to the hospital. When the nurses and doctors ask how, we say, a kitchen accident. If they demand more, we say, a chopping accident.

Nobody ever told me this—what to talk about and what not to talk about, what to say when a stranger asks a question. I learned it from observation. I learned it so young, I never thought about it at all, not until recently when my younger brother, barely eight years old, barely half my age, became a knife for the first time.

I'd seen my father and my older brothers become knives too many times to count. I'd seen them cut, felt their cuts. I'd kept quiet. I'd bandaged my wounds.

But my little brother—I'd changed his diapers, scrubbed dirt from beneath his fingernails. Once I'd held him in my arms all day long because he'd had strep and a fever. I'd rubbed circles into his back until my shoulder felt rusted.

When he turned into a knife, something in me unraveled. A spool of thread spun down to the bone. When he cut me, I howled loud and long.

Everyone stopped what they'd been doing and stared.

Then the knives and the not-knives all spoke at once. Told me to shut my mouth. Quit making a fuss.

Parts We Can Live Without

On Easter Sunday morning the year I turned eleven, I witnessed my Great Aunt Sarah come back to life from the dead. Before, inert in her wheelchair, she'd seemed no more sentient than a sack of groceries. I'm ashamed to admit that I'd complained right in front of her that she smelled like cheese.

But when a lizard fell as though from the sky and landed on Great Aunt Sarah's chest, she screamed and shook.

My sister Lucy and I and our cousins were scavenging Grandma Ellen's backyard for plastic eggs stuffed with chocolates and coins. Even cousin Webber, my prime competition in the Easter egg hunt, froze and stared. Great Aunt Sarah kept on screaming and shaking long after Grandma Ellen brushed the lizard off her. What calmed her eventually was Grandma Ellen taking her hands and singing "You Are My Sunshine."

*

Later, after we returned home, Dad caught three of our white laying hens and hung them by their necks from the chain-link fence. He said we had more eggs than we needed, so we might as well trade some eggs for meat.

The hens, which we'd raised from chicks, were alive and squawking.

Lucy, who was only five, plucked several of her own eyelashes before I noticed and took her hands in my own.

Lucy said, "Couldn't we take just some of the hens' meat and let them go without hurting them?"

Dad laughed and explained to Lucy that meat is muscle. To take only some of the hens' meat and release them would be far crueler than killing them.

"These chickens have lived good lives," he said. "And they're getting good deaths, too. They'll die quickly. They won't suffer."

In the laundry room, where we watched through the screen door as Dad untied the first hen and carried her to the chopping block, I told Lucy about Mike the Headless Chicken, who'd been famous for surviving eighteen months after his beheading. The farmer's blade left the brain stem intact. I read about it at the public library while Mom Jazzercised.

"You don't need your whole brain to live," I said. "All you need is the stem."

And a face. Mike had gone right on trying to peck and preen, but without his beak he would have died if the farmer hadn't fed and watered him with a dropper.

Mike spent the rest of his life touring the country. The farmer made a fortune from people paying a quarter each to see Mike with their own eyes. This was a long time ago, when Grandma Ellen and Great Aunt Sarah were girls, I told Lucy.

"Did Grandma and Great Aunt Sarah go to see him?" she asked.

I was too slow to stop her from plucking another eyelash.

"I don't know," I said.

I also didn't know if Mike had lost his brain before or after Great Aunt Sarah lost part of her brain. Unlike Mike, Great Aunt Sarah still had her face, but inside there, whole chunks were as good as missing. It was called a lobotomy. When she was eighteen, a doctor had poked an ice pick into the front of her brain and mashed the tissue like it was banana he was going to make into sweet bread, Mom said when I asked her what was wrong with Great Aunt Sarah.

Mom said doctors had thought lobotomy cured mental illness, meaning they'd thought Great Aunt Sarah had been sick in the head.

Of course, Great Aunt Sarah, who lived in a home for people who couldn't care for themselves, didn't seem cured of anything.

"Perhaps she made a lot of noise before," Mom said. "Men back then didn't like women to make too much noise."

*

As Dad lifted the blade above the neck of the first hen, all three hens seemed to squawk louder. Lucy pressed her palms tight against her ears. She looked like she might crush her skull.

After the blade came down, the hen's body writhed beneath Dad's grip. Like Great Aunt Sarah that morning.

Lucy asked, "Is it still alive?"

"No," I said, but I knew that wasn't the whole truth. I'd read that bodies shudder right after they die because the nerves still carry electric signals. Not only that, outer skin cells, which get much of their oxygen from air rather than blood anyhow, could survive several days.

Death didn't happen in one fell swoop. When the headless hen's wriggling stopped, and Dad lowered the body into the scalding water to loosen the feathers, parts of the hen were still alive.

There'd been no question Great Aunt Sarah had been alive when that lobotomist had taken some of her meat. But after she calmed down Easter morning, she looked once again as dead as that hen in the water, despite that her eyes were open wide.

Of course, appearances could be deceiving. A magician once called me onto stage for the levitation trick. I'd felt the table beneath me the entire time, but Lucy argued when I told her. She'd seen me levitate.

As Dad lifted the hen from the water, I wondered what Great Aunt Sarah could feel that we couldn't see. That scream hadn't been a postmortem shudder. What other impulses were still alive inside her, but missing components needed to carry them out? Like Mike trying to peck and preen despite the absence of his beak.

I didn't say any of this to Lucy.

Instead, I watched her closely as Dad yanked feathers from the hen's body. When my sister lifted her hand to her eyelashes again, I grabbed her hand just in time.

But my small triumph meant nothing to the hens on the fence.

A Treatise on the Broken Heart Idiom

Bea presented to her classmates a drawing of an ancient Egyptian priest inserting a long bronze hook through a corpse's nose. The task of the hook was to smash and dislodge brain matter. Like removing clumps of hair and sludge from a clogged drain.

Ancient Egyptians believed that the brain was nothing more than a snot factory. The heart was, in fact, the only internal organ that they left intact.

The idiom Bea had chosen to present on was "broken heart," as in the following examples spoken by her mother: "Your father broke my heart," "A broken heart never *really* mends," and, most recently, "My broken heart can't take one more blow."

"Of course," Bea said to her peers, "we've known for several hundred years now that the Egyptians had it all wrong. The brain is the center of intelligence and feeling. But still people go on and on about their broken hearts. Why broken?"

She showed the class a second image, this one the hieroglyph for heart. It was a jug with handles. A piece of pottery.

Not long after Bea's father left, her mother had said one morning, "*You're* breaking my heart, too."

Bea had said, "How can I break your heart if he already broke it?"

But now she pictured scattered shards of clay crumbling into grit beneath her sneakers. The pieces could be ground smaller and smaller until they were molecules, then atoms, then subatomic particles.

Ancient Egyptians believed one's heart was one's admission to the afterlife, but only if it passed a test: The heart was to be weighed against the feather of truth. If the heart was lighter than the feather, then Osiris deemed the individual worthy of the afterlife. If the heart was heavier than the feather, then Ammut, a demoness who was part lion, part hippopotamus, and part crocodile, would crush the corrupt muscle between her crocodilian teeth.

Crocodiles chomped down with as much as 16,000 newtons of force, Bea had read—the strongest bite ever measured by scientists. To compare, a lion bit down with only about 4,000 newtons of force. The ancient Egyptians had given the demoness the most fearsome chops they could imagine.

As a finale to her presentation, Bea triggered the mousetrap she'd set up earlier, a pottery shard the prey.

There was a loud snap. Pieces flew from the table. A few of her peers screamed.

Her teacher held out a dustpan.

What Bea didn't share with the class was that hieroglyphics always showed Osiris welcoming the deceased into the underworld. She couldn't find even one depiction of Ammut gnashing hearts in her powerful jaws.

Of course, no human heart was really lighter than a feather.

The journey to the afterlife was like the corn maze Bea's parents had taken her to one Halloween. The entrance had been flanked by a dozen signs warning of treachery, but other than Bea's parents nipping at each other like brute beasts, the maze had been tame as a goldfish.

Fish Story

after Donald Barthelme

Mrs. Lark is dying. I think it's the children. They're like an algal bloom polluting her water. What I know is that when I lived with her all those years in her yellow-walled apartment, Mrs. Lark seemed healthy. Then in August, she scooped me into a plastic bag and brought me here. She said to me, "I'll bet you didn't know I used to teach. That was long before your time. It's been fifteen years since I've been in the classroom!"

Before the children arrived, Mrs. Lark hummed as she painted alphabet letters the size of the children's skulls, each letter flanked by animals from axolotls with their pompous purple plumes to a zebu, the hump on the zebu's back like a giant leach draining fluid from its spine.

Now she cries in the afternoons after the children assemble themselves into the shape of a sea snake and slither out the door. She cries some mornings, too, before the children arrive. Like their coming and going is what's making her sick.

Or maybe it's her fruitless struggle to shield the children from the brutal facts of life that gets to her. She tries to focus them on inconsequential things. The alphabet, for instance. The first time she cried was the day the children complained about the alphabet posters she'd painted and pinned to the walls back in August. The children said, "H is for honeybee?! Are you not aware that honeybees are nearly extinct? What century do you live in?" The posters came down.

I won't lie; I was pleased to see the axolotls go.

But poor Mrs. Lark: slime oozed from her nostrils for an alarming length of time.

Children have the fidelity of hermit crabs. Trust me; I know. When the children first arrived, Mona, the one who glides (almost aquatic, that child), pointed at me and yelled, "Fish!" The children smashed their faces up against the glass of my tank like a brood of algae eaters. Not one minute later, the children had scattered like reef dwellers when a shark approaches. Their only interest in me since has been when Mrs. Lark asks, "Who wants to feed Chunk?" and every arm shoots up at once. Synchronize, synchronize.

Personally, I enjoy the lack of attention. When the children linger sometimes, after they shake the flakes into my tank, I eat too fast. I get indigestion. (If I don't eat immediately, Mrs. Lark decides I've been overfed. She scoops the flakes out with a net.)

Mrs. Lark cried, too, the day the children asked why the cat in the beginning-readers books is always described as fat. They said, "Why does the author not emphasize some other attribute, say the cat's shiny fur or wily character?" She said, "I guess because those words don't rhyme." The children said, "Is rhyming so essential that it trumps civility?" Mrs. Lark blushed. She said, "Of course, not."

A shameful oversight on her part, for sure. However, the irony of the children electing to rechristen me "Chunk," and some of them calling me "The Inimitable Chunka-Lunky Butthead Supreme" when Mrs. Lark isn't within hearing, is not lost on me, I'll tell you.

Then there was the day that the children asked about the framed watercolor hanging next to the classroom door. "What does it say?" they asked. "Don't settle for the second highest peak," Mrs. Lark read. The picture showed a man scaling a mountain, a rainbow overhead. The children said, "What if we want to climb the second highest peak?" Mrs. Lark said, "Oh, it's not meant so literally." The children said, "Is it not instructing us that the second highest peak is not worthy of our ambitions?" Mrs. Lark said, "Well." The children said, "What kind of message does this send to Mona? She can't climb any peaks at all." Mrs. Lark looked as though she'd been stunned by an electric eel.

Mrs. Lark has not scaled any peaks, I'm quite sure. She knows as well as I do, I believe, that life is about survival;

then you die. This mission of hers to try to convince the children otherwise is noble, I suppose, but foolhardy. She may hide her crying from them, but she can't hide how she's thinned these last several months. She can't hide how she's wilted, like the plant in my tank.

Today, after the children return from recess, Mrs. Lark holds up a ladle and says that the children will scoop water from one bowl into another and count the scoops. "Why?" the children ask. "I'm teaching you about nonstandard units of measurement," Mrs. Lark says. Her skin is pale, her dress wrinkled.

The children say, "If you were to write a book about the wisdom you have acquired over the course of your life, would there be a chapter on nonstandard units of measurement?"

Mrs. Lark coughs. "No, there would be no such chapter, but you are children. You have your whole lives to seek other lessons."

"Like what?" they ask.

Mrs. Lark stares at the floor. She's close now. Three days in a row, the children have shaken out more flakes than I can eat, and Mrs. Lark hasn't noticed. The water is so cloudy that the children are like floaters at the edges of my vision.

Mrs. Lark says, "How about you decorate the classroom walls with your art?"

The children run to the art station. They draw animals and authority figures, everything pooping or eating poop or shaped like poop. The children seem satisfied.

But sitting at her desk, Mrs. Lark looks limper than ever. Like when my fins stumble, and for a moment, I sink. My muscles feel so paltry. Death is taking nips out of us, devouring us slowly, bite by bite. If the plant in my tank is any indication, soon we will be nothing but mush. Mrs. Lark won't be writing any books, but pay attention, children, and you will learn all you need to know.

Lessons

In the shed, Ellen's mother presents a hammer for her to examine. "A hammer is a lever, a simple machine. All simple machines reduce the pushing or pulling force needed to move a load by increasing the distance over which that force must be applied," she says.

Ellen slides a finger around the cold metal knob and along the thick claws. She recalls the purple hammer birds in *Alice in Wonderland*, how their heads seemed backwards. The claw end of a hammer more closely resembles a beak, after all; but in the movie, the knobs are the birds' beaks, the claws like feathered hair moussed back. Of course, in the movie, the birds wedge nails into wood rather than pry them out as her mother does now.

"See how I lift the handle all the way up to remove the nail? I'm willing to work for a longer period of time so that I may apply less effort over the short-term. In the end, conservation of energy always prevails: input equals output. But most people don't appreciate how wildly different that input can be made to look and feel."

As is the case with most of her mother's lessons, Ellen understands that this one is at least partly about Ellen's father. Since he left them, he has remarried; fathered two boys, brothers Ellen has never met; and published a book of cookie recipes, three of which Ellen's mother claims he stole from her.

When they bake, Ellen's mother says that Ellen shouldn't believe the nonsense in cookbooks about how it's important to measure ingredients carefully. "I eyeball everything," her mother says. "It makes you wonder about people if they think baking is difficult."

Ellen pictures her father's new life as a tower her mother will dismantle, one nail at a time.

Now Ellen's mother lifts the wood from which she removed the nail. "Know how this can be used as a simple machine?"

Ellen shakes her head.

Her mother sets the wood onto the workbench and props up one end with a plastic tub of irrigation supplies. She places a box of nails at the other end.

"Imagine this box is really heavy. Push it up an inclined plane, and I can lift it without lifting it. The gentler the incline, the easier the load is to move, only I have to push the load longer. Not a bad trade-off, no? But most people are lazy. They'd risk throwing out their backs to be done faster."

Ellen's grandmother said her mother should "Take him to court," "Make him pay." But her mother said, "Let him sleep like the hare. Let him think he's won."

That made her mother the tortoise, who moves slowly because it carries armor on its back. What her mother plans to do when she catches up with the hare, Ellen doesn't know, but she knows this: there will be a lesson.

Cubist Mother

When I found my mother throwing dishes at the mortar wall behind our house, she said only, "I forgot these once belonged to my mother." In her hand was the pale blue dish, speckled like a bird's egg. Once upon a time, I'd stamped my feet if anyone else ate from it. Watching my mother hurl that dish, I thought of that Duchamp painting, *Nude Descending a Staircase, No. 2*. The curves of the figure's hips and buttocks, the metronomic swing of her legs and arms—all multiplied. Or is she disassembled? Shattered like a dish thrown against a wall.

Dendrochronology

When the knock sounds, she knows she's not to open the door. Her father has warned about these woods and their inhabitants. The expedience with which the knock travels through the little house reminds her that she is alone in a box made *of* wood. She has always liked boxes—the neatness of their borders, how they can be closed then opened then closed again. Her body is not so neat. Her father says, Keep your hands to yourself. Keep your mouth shut. Keep your legs closed. But right now, her body is sweaty because she is punctured with holes too small to see, and despite her concentration, despite saying to herself over and over, *close your pores and stop sweating*, she cannot close them. She is *full of* holes, she thinks. *Full of* is strange language when what you're talking about is holes, which are full of nothing but empty space. Then again, empty space isn't truly empty; it contains air, which is made up of invisible particles; and these particles contain still more particles. Nothing is ever quite as it appears. Like these woods, which she realizes she has always imagined as a box she could be shut up inside of. But is she not a container for the woods, too? The way her imagination has nurtured this idea of the woods as a fanged box, watered it and fertilized it? The way she has cultivated the idea that the creature on the other side of the wood door is a monster that means to eat her up? Through the peephole she studies the wolf's fluffy face, notices the urge she feels to reach out and pet that thick, soft fur. Would she be able to comb her fingers all the way through to the skin, to the pores? Would the wolf's skin feel sweaty, like her own? If only she could be sure the creature really were a wolf, perhaps then she would open that door. Perhaps she would climb upon the wolf's back and ride far away from here. But she worries that all that fur is a mask. She worries her father is hiding in there somewhere, her father who has taught her to fear these woods, to fear this wolf, to never ever open the door. The woods and all they contain have nothing to do with her, he has said, he who went out to those woods this afternoon, who goes out to the woods many afternoons and mornings and evenings—to chop wood for the fire, to catch meat for their meals, to score fur for their bedding; he who will punish her severely if he catches her so much as putting her hand on this knob.

Bargain

When I was fourteen, I babysat for a couple with three gorgeous kids, two girls and a boy. The kids' mother was a ballerina. She was petite and muscular. The kids' father seemed to me like a bear, he was so much bigger than her. And because there was something foreboding about him. I imagined he contained a dark forest inside his skin. He was handsome, though. The few times he was the one to relay instructions to me about dinner and bedtime while the kids' mother finished getting ready behind their closed bedroom door, I couldn't look him in the eye.

I didn't know much back then, but I knew the couple was drunk when they returned late at night. They had a ragged sloppiness about them, like clothes wrinkled from sitting too long in the dryer. How late, I don't remember now, only that they stayed out much later than my parents ever did. If my parents went out, it was for chicken fried steak and a movie. They were in bed by ten.

When the couple returned, the kids' father handed me a wad of crumpled dollar bills. I was grossly underpaid. A bargain, my friend Steph called me. The family she babysat for lived in a house with ceilings so high she couldn't reach them with a broomstick. Two kids versus the three in my charge, but her hourly rate was three times what the Elliots paid me.

I put up with it because I told myself they wouldn't be able to afford dates if it weren't for me. Their house was small. Some of the tiles had come up in the kitchen. Every room looked like an unfinished craft project.

Also, I was frugal. Scolded my younger siblings when they begged our mother for toys at the store. Got scolded by her in return because our mother was not frugal. Years later, after my parents divorced, she would blow through her half of their savings within two years, despite having a full-time job and no health problems or other financial impediments.

I put up with it too because I was timid and eager to please, thus easy to take advantage of, which is to say I wasn't a particularly good babysitter. The Elliots got what they paid for.

The kids' father always drove me home. The kids' mother muttered thank you, then disappeared into their bedroom. The glow that had been in her cheeks on the way out the door was dulled and hardened when they walked back in.

Without a word, he would hold the front door for me, just as he had for her some hours earlier.

The drive wasn't far—a couple miles. Still, he never said a word about how maybe he shouldn't drive me home, how maybe he'd had too much to drink.

Of course, I could have said something. I could have called and woke my father to tell him to come get me. But I didn't. Just like how a few years later, I wouldn't speak up in so many other circumstances involving men who would make me feel as small and inconsequential as a gnat. As that bear of a man drove in silence, as though he were alone, I felt so much smaller than his ballerina wife, smaller even than his children. In truth, I was taller than all of them, but I didn't own my height. I didn't own anything about my body other than my shame at being the kind of girl no one gave a damn about, not even a man with alcohol on his breath, nothing but crumpled ones in his pocket.

Sockets

The rush of water through the tub faucet is like ants when they find something dead. My grandmother is in her bathroom, the too-small door shut as tight as it will shut. I'm on the gritty floor of the hall closet, wedged in next to the vacuum canister. I'm watching how the light at the bottom of the bathroom door flickers like flames as my grandmother shuffles around in there. I can stack two fingers beneath that door. My little sister, Dell, can stack three.

I'd like to pull closed the closet door, but I don't dare. Last time, Dell lit her hair on fire. The long, brown strands had burned to within a few inches of her scalp when my naked, dripping grandmother doused Dell's head with a wet bath towel. My grandmother no longer leaves lit candles in the living area when she bathes, but still.

With a shortbread cookie, I try to coax Dell into the closet with me. So I can keep her safe for a little while. Also, because I like how when Dell nestles in my lap, she pinches the thin skin on the insides of my arms. Pinches as hard as she can. "You need this medicine, or you'll die," she says.

But Dell snatches the bait and scurries away. Her left profile facing me, I can't see what she calls "the boy half of her head." Squatting in her pilled cotton nightgown, her toenails overgrown and jagged, her girl half looks scavenger.

I know my grandmother has stepped into the water because the plunge of her foot makes a terrible, hand-reaching-into-your-chest-to-fist-your-heart sound as the water gives way, wedges open. I think of the diagram our mother showed Dell and me of a sperm wriggling its way into an oocyte, the name for a human egg. Not really an egg, but so called because of its roundabout resemblance, as things often are. Our mother said a sperm swims a long distance to get to an oocyte, like swimming from one continent to another, she said. The way she talked about sperm, you'd think they were rippled with muscles. But the sperm in the picture looked to me like a single flower bud of broccoli with its thread stem, the oocyte a hungry head.

The lesson on fertilization was our mother's segue into telling us she and her boyfriend, Jeffrey, were going to have a baby together. But the conclusion was obvious from the start, what with the weird way she patted the worn sofa cushion on either side of her and told Jeffrey to snap photos of the three of us looking at that library book. It was like when Dell tries to tell a joke, but she accidently announces the punchline before she's completed her setup.

Dell's too young to know about the before of the sperm and the oocyte, but she's heard the sounds our mother and Jeffrey made behind our mother's bedroom door, back before our mother ran off with Jeffrey and left us with our grandmother. "I'll be back soon," our mother said thirteen weeks ago, dragging a little blue suitcase crammed with her favorite dresses and a white bikini I hadn't even known she owned. They were going to the beach for a few days, she said. R and R, she said.

The cookie all gone, Dell wets her thumb and ferries crumbs from the floor to her mouth. Each thumb strike against the wooden planks sounds like a bug being squished.

I want to suck up every sound in my grandmother's house with the vacuum, make all the vibrations vanish, but I'm afraid to plug the vacuum into the outlet. Electricity licks from those holes like a tongue when our grandmother plugs in some appliance. Our grandmother says she should call an electrician, but she never does. Most of what our grandmother talks about has to do with things she ought to do but doesn't and won't. Like buy new vacuum bags—the vacuum's been empty since our mother left. Like hunt down our mother and drag her back here.

I picture our mother a limp doll, dragged by a single raggedy, batting-stuffed arm.

Electricity sticks out its tongue because it's excited about the incoming plug, our grandmother said one afternoon as she plugged in the immersion blender. She was making broccoli-cheese soup, which she told us used to be our mother's favorite. When Dell stuck out her tongue to mean the opposite of excitement, our grandmother said, "You'll eat it then because I made it and because it's good for you."

The flat, white faces in the wall don't look excited, either. Their features sunken in like the clay portrait Dell made of our mother in preschool a few days ago (a gift for Mother's Day), poking holes for the eyes and mouth and nose, they look sad-surprised, as though they've inadvertently driven over a kitten and felt the crunch of its bones beneath the tires. When I told Dell eyes aren't holes, she said, "But they're called eye *sockets* and eye *balls.*" When I said, "OK, but where are the eyeballs?" she said, "Vacation. Duh."

I think electricity is just lonely.

And I think it would like to flow through me and Dell and our grandmother as much as through any appliance. Like that fire excitedly climbing Dell's hair. Dell said those flames were like the prince in the story of Rapunzel: they climbed her hair to get to the rest of her.

A body is water more than anything else. My teacher showed us a diagram of a girl and boy, both filled to their shoulders with blue liquid, like partially used bottles of perfume. Maybe that's why people like my grandmother and my mother like to soak in the tub so much. The water inside draws them to the water outside. Their water brain, like how the stomach is a second brain, lined with more neurons than even the spine.

Electricity wants to be wrapped up inside water, too, which is why you must be careful not to let them near each other. Electricity will hurl itself into water fast as anything.

Everything just wants to be wrapped up inside something.

Like how our mother said about Jeffrey that being with him makes her feel as cozy and secure as a body in a coffin. "Like there isn't anything I need other than him."

I think I know what she means. The vacuum closet is like that. In the dark, I press my ear against the hollow canister pillow. I cast myself into its clean emptiness. My grandmother's house doesn't just feel far away. It's like nothing outside that vacuum is real.

A Girl Scout Is Useful, Thrifty, Cheerful, Courteous, Clean in Thought, and, Above All, Loyal*

This does not mean she thinks her family is perfect, far from it. She knows they are breeding places of disease.

She keeps her family clean, neat, and in good repair. Removes crumbs from the skin of their necks, dust and litter from their eyes. Leaves nothing in their mouths between meals. She uses boiling water, and plenty of it, to flush their throats. She brings air and sunlight into their dark and dirty places.

---

* Collage comprised of words and phrases from *Scouting for Girls: Official Handbook of the Girl Scouts*, 1925.

If grime does get lodged in their throat or their stomach, the family member may be governed by a mad instinct to grab anything which subconsciously they think may save their life. A stained person is always a frightened person.

But the girl knows something of ropes and knots. She fastens their arms, legs, fingers. Pulls tight.

Skilled at retrieving objects at a reasonable depth from the surface, she ties a rope around her body and ties the other end to some sturdy piece of furniture, such as a stove or refrigerator. She washes her hands thoroughly. Carries a knife in diving. When she finds the speck, she scrapes it into an old tin box. Climbs out by way of the ladder of the spine.

In some cases, the source of disease may be in their heads. The girl grasps the family member by the eyelashes. Pulls the eyelid free of the ball. She looks for the best in them. Her belief in them may be the very thing they need most.

Hostages

The hostages, though they can't speak through the fat strips of silver duct tape, nonetheless seem to communicate. I don't mean anything concrete, like an escape plan. One of them gets a scared look in her eyes, and another one mirrors the look back, like how Mom reflected my anger two days ago when I told her about how Kyra tripped me at recess, hence the scratches on my chin and palms. "That girl is a bully," Mom said. Then she softened. She said people who treat others like that aren't okay inside. She said Kyra probably has "a rough home life," and I pictured walls, floors, and furniture all scratchy as sandpaper.

The hostages are not strangers to each other the way the hostages in a movie I saw once were—random people who happened to be in the same place at the same time. These hostages are coworkers—Dad's coworkers. Ex-coworkers, since he was fired last week. There are twenty-seven of them, the number of kids in my fifth-grade class minus me. I make twenty-eight, but I'm not a hostage.

This isn't my first time at Dad's office, so I recognize a lot of the hostages. One of them I know by name. Judith keeps a stash of little toys in her purse for doling out to other people's children. She's a no-frills Santa Claus. On visits to Dad's office, Judith has given me the following toys: a pouch containing eight tiny colored pencils; a calculator with neon green buttons; a plastic cockroach that skitters forward on little wheels after you roll it backwards and let go.

Now Judith looks at me pleadingly as though I might help her. Or maybe she's feeling sorry for me because I'm a kid who is witness to her dad taking hostages.

The word "hostages" makes me think of the word "sausages." I think of those tiny pig-in-a-blanket sausages that come in shrink-wrapped packs, squeezed up against each other not unlike Dad's ex-coworkers are now. In the small conference room, only six chairs fit around the circular table. Of course, the hostages are not seated at the table. They're crammed in against each other around the perimeter of the room. They're also like a string of sausages, only side-to-side rather than end-to-end.

A hostage situation I didn't see on TV but heard about because I was up listening when my parents thought I was asleep involved Mom. A gunman entered an office where she'd worked, before I was born, and he'd taped her and her coworkers' mouths shut, too, just like Dad did to his ex-coworkers minutes ago. Mom didn't sound scared telling Dad about this. She sounded perplexed. "Do you know what scared me most? I was terrified that man was going to rape me in front of my coworkers. I worked in an office that was all men. I was the only woman. It wasn't the fear of death or even rape itself that got to me. It was the humiliation of being raped in front of those guys."

Dad said, "Jesus."

Now Dad doesn't say anything. He stands in the doorway, his hunting rifle pointed at the wall a few feet above Judith's head. He scrunches up his shoulders like he's got an ache in his back or his neck. I look in at Judith and the others through the glass wall, warming that glass with my breath.

Dad isn't just mad at them, for still having jobs, or for being responsible somehow for his not having a job; he's mad at me, too, for having been on the floorboard in the back of his car without his knowing it, and on a school day; and for sneaking into the building, finding him in this situation. Of course, I hadn't known this was what I'd find. I'd hoped to get another toy out of Judith even though I'm too old for such things now, at the age of eleven. I'd hoped to feel comforted by Judith's eagerness to make me smile. I'd hoped to feel a little less worried about going back to school.

Most of all, I think Dad's mad I'm observing his poor role modeling.

That's a thing Mom is always saying to Dad—that he needs to be a better role model for me. Every time I ask for something—a glass of juice, a new tube of toothpaste—without saying, "please," he says, "How do you ask nicely?" Mom echoes his question when a few minutes later he inevitably asks, or tells, her to do something without asking nicely himself. Another thing that gets her going is when he says to me, "You're making me angry" or "If you do ____, I'm not going to be happy." Mom says, "She's not responsible for your feelings, Andy."

I try to think what Mom would say now. On top of everything else wrong with this picture, she wouldn't approve of the shirt he's wearing. She says it smells like sauerkraut; she says the smell is locked in and it's time to let that shirt go.

This is the same language Dad's boss, ex-boss, used with him. "I have to let you go, Andy." I wonder which one of these people is Dad's ex-boss. Four of the men wear long-sleeved shirts and ties as opposed to the polo shirts the other men wear, so I'm guessing one of them. Also, the tie men's eyes are a different kind of startled than everyone else's. Like Kyra yesterday when I cornered her in the girls' bathroom just as the bell that signaled the end of the school day rang, a rock in my hand triple the size of my fist.

I recognize the look in Dad's eyes, too. The realization that he's made a horrible mistake, that there will be repercussions, and those repercussions will find him no matter where he goes.

Hail Satan

The year our parents took us out of church school, because with Lily starting kindergarten they could no longer afford tuition, Mrs. Pyrtle warned Mom that public school would expose us to terrible evils. Carrie and I overheard Mom tell Dad this as he helped her unload groceries from the trunk of her car. "She said they're going to wind up taking candy from the hands of Satan."

Mom was prone to exaggeration. Complain about her meatloaf, and she'd act like you said you'd rather flames from the stove lick her like she was a spitted chicken than politely eat what she'd prepared. So maybe she misrepresented Mrs. Pyrtle's warning, but the point is that by the time that big yellow bus came to a screeching stop in front of our house for the first time, Carrie and I were on the lookout for Satan.

We found Satan everywhere in public school. Satan was in the cafeteria, where the girls asked us if our mother sewed our clothes. Satan was on the school bus, where the older kids called us pussies when we wouldn't hang our heads out the windows as the bus scraped against tree limb after tree limb. Satan was most definitely at recess, where classmates goaded us to play a game called Butt Ball, the objective of which seemed to be to pelt us with such fury, it pained us to sit.

But our younger sister Lily, who wasn't the new kid, the weird church-school kid, who hadn't heard what Mrs. Pyrtle had said, seemed perfectly at ease. On the school bus, she sat with three other girls her age. With their hair bows and their charm bracelets and their sequined tops, they looked like fancy bonbons in a four-piece box. As Carrie and I watched Lily smile all the way to school and back, we decided that she was so full of Satan's candy, she was like a piñata. What she needed was to be busted open with a stick.

We prescribed all sorts of fixes, from prayers to dabbing cod liver oil behind her ears to not washing her hair. We believed we meant to save our sister. Like that time at the beach when we told her about saltwater crocodiles. How were we to know they weren't lurking in that muddy Gulf water?

Soon, Lily sat alone on the bus. She stared quietly out the window as the bus weaved in and out of ugly neighborhoods like a worm tunneling through manure. Lily prayed as the candy girls whispered about her from two seats up.

Then, one day one of the girls called out to Lily, "What's your deal?" as the other girls snickered. And Lily, naïve Lily, told them about her efforts to ward off Satan. She said she would pray for them, too.

In an instant, all eyes were on Lily.

It was like Butt Ball. Lily was spread against the wall, and she was looking over her shoulder at Carrie and me, begging, "Tell them. Tell them!"

We seemed to have two choices, either peg her in the butt as hard as we could or spread against the wall alongside her. But damn if our poor butts weren't already bruised enough.

Before After

In the before: a spider dangling from a bare branch, the sun. In the after: a luminous web, the moon. The latter is pale yellow and has a solitary dimple like the spot where an orange is ripped from its pedicel.

These illustrations are from a wordless book of paired images that the girl's father sent for the girl's tenth birthday, not grasping that the girl is too old for picture books.

Before, a quill pen and a bottle of ink. After, a typewriter. Before, a cave painting of a cow. After, an oil painting of a cow.

Before sleep—that's when the girl and the mother look at the book. The mother turns the pages. The girl tells the story of the before and after.

The girl understands what story the spider pictures are intended to tell, but she thinks, too, of what the mother said recently about how people may one day have to live on the moon. Because people may destroy Earth. Because people are stupid and greedy.

"I'd rather die than go to the moon," the girl said.

The mother said, "Surely that's not true." Then she said she hadn't meant to worry the girl. She was just thinking out loud.

The mother often spoke to the girl of subjects that then worried the girl: formaldehyde in furniture, elephant poaching, what happens to the body during menopause.

Later in the book, there is a series of houses—a house of straw, a house of wood, a house of brick. In the before, the first two houses lack doors and windowpanes. In the after, these houses have fallen apart. In the after for the house made of brick, the house's previously open doors and windows are shut tight. The house stands.

When the girl does not offer up a story, the mother says, "Progress, see? This house is stronger. The wolf can't destroy it. He can't get inside, either."

"But everything can be destroyed," the girl says.

"That's not how the story goes," the mother says.

"What if the wolf becomes stronger, too?" The girl thinks of how she has smote webs with only a flick of her hand.

"Nonsense. The wolf would give up and go after a pig that is easier to capture," her mother says.

"What if this is the last pig on Earth? The wolf has eaten all the other pigs."

The girl's mother opens her mouth, but the girl continues. "So the wolf huffs with the force of a tornado. Or the wolf tears down the house with a wrecking ball. Or the wolf puts on a gas mask, poisons the air. Or the wolf nukes the house."

Why Science Lessons That Involve Potatoes Give Me Grief

Kindergarten: Germination

Because before we planted our potatoes, we were instructed to give them faces—red smiles and googly eyes. Because potatoes are alive, dormancy like a deep sleep. Because a nurse likened my sister to a vegetable rather than, say, a stone. Because before this same nurse unplugged the heart-lung machine, my sister had lain as still and quiet as Snow White. Because despite the face I'd given it, my potato, inert on my desk, did not look alive either. Because later when my potato laid face-up in a hole I'd dug in the school garden, dropping handfuls of dirt onto its phony face felt like murder. Because men in gray suits sealed my sister inside a wooden box, like a time capsule. Because the teacher talked about the knobby buds, also called eyes, from which roots would grow. Because I pictured my sister sprouting—curly tendrils emerging from the scabbed mosquito bites that had dotted her legs. Because I wondered would her roots push through the wood, seek water?

Fourth Grade: Circuits

Because as I inserted nails and wire into my potato's skin, I thought of tracheotomies I'd seen performed on television. Because as I connected the wires, I thought of heart defibrillators shocking the dead back to life. Because before the nurse unplugged the heart-lung machine, my sister had lain as still and quiet as Snow White. Because my sister's brain had been like a broken circuit. Because when the bulbs blinked on, the teacher talked about phosphoric acid and hydrogen ions. Because I couldn't see ions. Because I stared at the light illuminating my potato's mottled skin. Because it was the opposite of Dr. Frankenstein's monster—light a product rather than a reactant. Because after class I read about the inspiration for Mary Shelley's book: Luigi Galvani making the legs of dead frogs twitch by zapping them with electricity. Because a girl in class said as she yanked the wires from her potato, Go to sleep now, so you can wake up fresh in the morning.

Seventh Grade: Newton's Second Law of Motion

Because the teacher told us to pretend that our foil-wrapped potatoes were astronauts and that the straws were space debris, like loose screws and washers from the International Space Station. Because an astronaut's suit is a dam. Because a tear could cause a body to swell, lungs to rupture, blood to boil. Because the pressure in space is too low for human survival. Because a friend of my mother's said that my sister was up in the sky looking down on me. Because the teacher instructed us to first nudge the straws at our potatoes gently, slowly, to notice how the straws collapsed upon impact. Because he then told us to jab the straws a little faster, harder, notice how the straws punctured the foil, then the skin. Because force is the product of mass and acceleration. Because even the tiniest objects can be deadly, if they move at great speeds. Because a bullet. Because duh. Because after the nurse unplugged the heart-lung machine, my sister had lain as still and quiet as Snow White. Because for dinner the night the nurse unplugged the machine, my mother cooked baked potatoes, also wrapped in foil, their skins sliced vertically like pillowcases unzipped. Because there were tiny holes in the foil and skin where my mother had poked a fork. Because too much pressure is as dangerous as too little pressure. Because skin is a dam, too. Because the holes felt like wounds after you pick away the scabs.

Dollhouse Furniture

The girl knows the little wooden piece her father sent for her birthday is supposed to be an oven range, because on top are four black burners the circumference of cigarette burns, and on the panel between the stovetop and the oven door are tiny, warty knobs. But the knobs do not turn. The oven does not heat up. The burners do not emit flames. Open the oven door, and there are two empty shelves like the shelves in the kitchen cabinet over their microwave, the cabinet where her father had kept his gin, before her mother told him one night as she was sponging up rings on the counters that their marriage was broken, and he said, "Broken? Can a thing be broken if it never worked to begin with?"

II

Phainopepla

Even before our brother poisoned us, we'd lived in the woods, only then we'd each been alone. We'd had to hunt and hide, to survive. It had been a difficult life, lonely. But we'd learned from our mother to trust no one.

Then our mother died, and our brother opened a window in the house where we all were born and called to us. "Sisters, you can come out now."

We weren't so sure. Our brother had lived with our mother all that time, after all. And none of us had seen each other in years.

But the heart wants, even when it knows better.

So, we crept back gingerly, rolling our feet softly on the earth, our eyes scanning for traps.

As we neared the house, the landscape shifted. The few remaining trees were studded with prickly balls of mistletoe. When they kissed the trees, they latched on and didn't let go. They bored inside the trunks, stole the trees' water.

Black birds with red eyes flitted among the trees. *Phainopepla.* They ate the mistletoe's berries and spread the sticky seeds from limb to limb by way of their shit.

Inside the house, we stared at one another, strangers. Then our brother introduced us. He pointed to our oldest sister, said, "You always thought you were smarter than the rest of us." To our second oldest sister, he said, "You always thought you were more special than the rest of us." To me, he said, "You were always cold and insensitive."

"What about you?" our oldest sister said.

He said, "I'm the one who cared for our poor, dear mother."

"Not so poor," our oldest sister said.

"Not so dear," the second oldest said.

A *Phainopepla* flew in through the open window then and dropped a white berry onto the black Formica. It looked like a pearl onion. Our brother tried to eat one once, at Christmas, when he was a toddler, but our mother slapped it from his hand, said they're poisonous.

The bird flew up to the rafters of the house. There hanging from the wooden beams were three balls of mistletoe in a neat row. White berries dotted the clumps like boils.

Our brother said, "Mother died of a broken heart."

Our oldest sister said, "I heard she died of cancer."

He said, "Your ingratitude tore a hole in her heart that let the cancer in." He picked up the berry, held it up for inspection, and smashed it between his fingertips.

I said, "A heart is a bloody fist. No more, no less."

Our brother announced it was time for dinner.

At the table, he ladled a white broth into four black bowls.

We were cautious. We waited for him to take the first bite. He did.

As we ate, he retold the story we'd all heard countless times: that our grandmother sent our mother into the woods alone when she was just a girl. Unbeknownst to Mother, Grandmother dispatched a wolf along after her, promised her to the wolf. But the wolf swallowing her was not the awful part, Mother always said. In fact, she was never so content as she was inside that wolf, and that's why Grandmother slit open the wolf's belly and wrestled Mother from him. Because she wanted Mother to have no pleasure in life.

Our brother said, "Betrayed by her mother, then betrayed by her daughters."

Our oldest sister laughed. She said, "The only thing I take from that story is that Mother hated us before we were even born."

Our second oldest sister said, "She drove us into the woods, too, you know, only we went voluntarily, because the woods were more hospitable than this place."

I said to our brother, "Why did you call us back here?"

Another *Phainopepla* flew into the house. It joined the first one in the rafters.

Years ago, when I left, our brother had been thirteen and wild. He put snakes in my bed, threatened me with knives. All that while, our mother coddled him and defended him. He's just a boy, she said.

I'd heard over the years that our brother had grown out of that wildness, as though it had been a skin he'd shed. But as I stared across the table into his eyes, which were beastly and rimmed in black, I saw that he'd discarded nothing. And how could he have? Thirty-two years he'd lived with our mother.

I knew then that he'd poisoned us. All these years, he'd been building his immunity, for this moment.

I said, "*You* always believed you were a victim. Just like Mother."

Now my sisters and I lay still on the damp earth as the trees tap our arteries. Drink us in. Balls of mistletoe hover above the husks of our bodies like unwieldy halos. I think I know now why Mother didn't try to escape when the black of the wolf's mouth stretched wider and wider to take the whole of her inside. It felt like love.

Fertilizer

When I was seventeen, men were always wanting to feed me. Steak, quiche, Big Macs, ice cream. They wanted to take me to restaurants, put stuff inside me. One man offered me chicken soup he'd made himself, and I swooned. I thought: this man truly cares for me. I ate that soup on his worn brown couch in front of his television. I don't remember what we watched, but I remember it was winter, the scratchy nubs of grass on his lawn frosted over. I remember I hadn't even finished that bowl of soup before he shucked my pants. I understood then the purpose of the soup: a garden won't feed you unless you feed it first. That man harvested all of me right there on the couch. I remember him telling me how good I tasted.

Three Ways to Eat Quince

When ripe, quince is knobby and hard, like bone. You could break a window with it. You could break your teeth. That's what Liza's boss at the market told her about the strange yellow fruits in the red crate the farmer's youngest boy had just delivered, along with every sort of gourd.

The previous Sunday the boy had put his spongy tongue in Liza's mouth beside the dumpster out back and squeezed her breasts as though they were stress-relief balls. She'd ached for days after.

Still, she would've let him do it again.

But the boy hadn't acknowledged Liza except to say "excuse me" as he pushed the dolly past the pumpkins. Like she was a customer—one of the crones who inspect every onion in the bin.

She didn't know what precisely the storeowner had seen, but as he jiggled one of the quince as though to guess what was inside, he watched Liza, as though to guess what was inside her, too.

"When fruits bruise," he said—his name was Mark or Mr. Sibley, but Liza was uncomfortable choosing, so she didn't call him anything, just waited until he noticed her before speaking—"they don't heal. Not like you and me. We can take all sorts of tumbles and be just fine given time. Fruit rots."

Liza blushed.

The storeowner looked away.

"The interesting thing about quince is that rotting sweetens them. It's called bletting."

Bletting sounded like shorthand for bloodletting.

As the storeowner pulled a box cutter out of his pocket and broke the fruit's skin, carving out two wedges, Liza half-expected him to cut himself. Maybe she wanted him to, for his blood to stain the fruit's white flesh pink.

His calloused fingers scraped her skin as he deposited a wedge of the woody fruit into her palm. It was hard as a stone.

"Smells sweet to me," Liza said.

The storeowner laughed. "Don't let the fragrance fool you. Ripe quinces are full of acids and tannins. Another way to eat them is to cook them down with tons of sugar. Membrillo. Had it?"

Liza shook her head.

"It's like candy. Still, some people do eat them raw. The farmer sucks on them. Dries his mouth out, he says. Should we try it?"

Liza thought about how the storeowner's fingers had been all over the quince. Sucking on it would be like admitting his fingers into her mouth.

He smiled good-naturedly, the way the farmer's boy had when he'd led her out to the dumpster.

Years later, she read that quince may have been what Adam and Eve ate, from the tree of knowledge of good and evil, and she recalled that Sunday morning—how the storeowner had hardly put the quince to his lips before he spit it out. "No, thank you. Give me membrillo."

Not Liza. She'd let the quince sink its teeth into her. She didn't even make a face.

An Arm or a Palm Frond or a Boot

The boy is making his rusty old truck do things the girl didn't know it could do when she sees an arm in the road. She knows better than to say anything in the moment. She keeps quiet as sap. Only after the boy parks the truck behind a thick tangle of trees, the road's presence detectable solely by the sirens that whoosh past, does she say, "I saw an arm in the road a few miles back. A man's arm."

The boy says nothing, stares straight ahead at the trees. His long, elegant fingers still grip the wheel. She told him once that his fingers are her favorite part of his body. He didn't like that so much. Didn't like how she compared his fingers to delicate spider legs, either. "A guy doesn't want to be told that any part of him is delicate," he said.

The girl says, "I guess it could have been a palm frond or a boot, but what I saw was a man's arm. Thick and rough and tan."

The boy's fingers tap the wheel. The movement of the bones beneath the thin skin make the girl think of ballerinas chassé-ing in pointe shoes.

He says, "Are you saying you think we should go back? You think we made a terrible mistake?"

The girl sees the fear in the boy's eyes, and she remembers their second date. She gave him a mix tape, and she complained that all he brought her was a dumb cereal box joke. But then he kissed her, like she was oxygen and he was asphyxiating. Other boys had only ever kissed her like she was helium.

When the girl's friend said he wasn't good enough for the girl and asked what the girl saw in him, the girl said, "I see gentleness in him, vulnerability. And I see that he tries to see me."

"Tries?" the friend said, shaking her head like the girl was the biggest fool she'd ever met.

"That's right," the girl said. "And that's more than I can say for you."

Now the girl takes the boy's hand in her hands, and she says, "I'm just telling you what I saw. Maybe I saw wrong. Maybe I didn't. Either way, I saw what I saw."

What We Expect to See

We're organizing the plush fanged bats in the cave gift shop by size and color, and Sheila is telling me about total cave darkness. She says people hallucinate. She says it's kind of like doing mushrooms.

No customers in almost two hours, on account of the monsoon. Driving to work this morning, I couldn't see more than a few yards ahead. The edges of things smudged and dissolved. I drove with my face pressed into the windshield.

The cave is the end of a road. Nothing beyond but saguaros and cholla and other prickly things. It's not a place you wander upon by accident. It's not a place you pass by on your way to someplace else.

When I told Sheila I graduated from college this past spring, she said, "How'd you end up here?" I shrugged. College had been like a cave I got turned around in. Everyone else went in one end and came out the other. Like my friend, Heather, who's living in New York City, working as a stagehand on Broadway while attending auditions. But me, I somehow came out the same way I went in, only instead of the hardware store, there's the cave gift shop; and instead of Steve, the pothead with the pregnant girlfriend, there's Bob, married and with three kids.

I've never actually been inside the cave, but I've heard plenty of stories from Sheila, like that a couple of bandits hid in there nearly a century earlier after a heist. Sheila believes the stolen gold is lost in there with their bones.

Even now, long after the Civilian Conservation Corps put in flooring and lights, it's easy to get lost in the cave, Sheila says.

But it's what she says about total darkness that gets me.

"The brain can't resist filling in that void, making a map. You see what you expect to see. The problem is you can be very wrong about what's there," Sheila says. There are seventy-foot drop-offs in the cave, she says. If you expect that floor lies beneath you where it does not, down you will go.

I think I would like to be mistaken about what's there. I mean I want to experience what presumably comes after, when light lifts that veil and you see that your surroundings are not as you had thought. Like the plays Heather performed in: the lights dimmed and when they came on again, the stage was transformed into something new.

According to Sheila, Felix is the best cave guide there is.

She says, "Never mind that weird glove he wears. He's like a subterranean rodent the way he can find his way out from deep underground without a pinch of light."

The glove in question is white and fuzzy, like a miniature sweater. It ends at the knobby tip of his ulna bone, where the ulna connects to the cobbled carpal bones of his wrist. Concealed by the glove, the tip of his ulna looks like a blindfolded eye. Perhaps an eye that is hypersensitive to sunlight, the way eyes get when they've been in total cave darkness for several days, their pupils dilated for hours on end.

People say that after three days in total darkness, you become blind, but Sheila says that's bullshit. Felix has spent days in there at a time, she says. There are monks who do it for years.

"How do they eat? Where do they shit?" I ask her.

Sheila shrugs.

When my shift ends, there is one tour remaining, and Felix is leading it. He stands before the entrance of the cave, a hole in the limestone the shape of a person wrapped in a bedsheet. The only other people signed up are two nuns, one short and one tall, both wearing full habits.

The cave is brighter than I expected. Lightbulbs are hidden beneath rock fixtures to illuminate the drop-offs Sheila spoke of. Like passing exit door after exit door.

When sitting in the exit rows of planes, I've sometimes felt the urge to turn the handle and push, to take everyone else down with me.

After snaking one-by-one through narrow passages, we come to what Felix calls a room. We're sixty feet below Earth's surface, and he says this is it. When he turns out the lights, we will experience pure darkness. But first, we must sit, he says, so we don't wander and plummet to our deaths. "I mean it. Keep still. You'd be surprised by how convincing hallucinations can be."

In the dark, the nuns talk excitedly about waving their hands in front of their faces and seeing a milky glimmer of motion, like the scattered specks of color when a hummingbird beats its wings.

What I experience is the clamminess of the cave air and the darkness that feels like the heavy lead blanket you wear during X-rays.

I see nothing. My brain offers no map.

I am calm, though. I think the darkness is a prelude.

But when Felix turns the lights on, everything looks the same as before. Nothing is transformed.

The nuns stand. They thank Felix and tell him they look forward to doing it again sometime.

I think about how there's so much people can't see that they nonetheless believe is there. Like God, like the bones shrouded by their flesh. Perhaps other people's brains offer maps where mine just stares dumbly at the void.

Or: maybe my whole life I've been navigating by a false map conjured by my brain.

I pound now at the rock beneath me until my knuckles hurt. I'm afraid to stand, afraid to take a step. How do I know that anything I see is real?

When Felix offers me his gloved hand and says, "It's okay. I'm right here," I want badly to believe his hand is real. I want badly to believe he can lead me out.

Feng Shui

Nisha is abandoning Lauren to move in with her boyfriend, Tim. She tells Lauren this in the crowded furniture store, where they wait for a free lecture about feng shui. A white paper plate loaded with sweaty cheese cubes and wet grapes rests on Lauren's lap. A few of the grapes are punctured, their gelatinous insides exposed, leaking out like they've been stabbed and left for dead. Nisha's lap is empty. She glanced at the food and said she wasn't hungry.

The flier Nisha brought home to their apartment last week read: *Change your environment; change your life.* Like something out of a fortune cookie. Nisha said, "You should come with me."

Before Lauren can respond to the news, the Feng Shui Guru stands and begins. He is short and tan, and his bald head gleams like an apple. He tells them that chi is the energy humming in all things, from a gust of wind to the atoms vibrating in place in the most static of objects.

Nothing is really still, he says. Only chi moves differently in different objects and spaces. The goal is to arrange their homes so as to balance their chi.

For instance, pillows absorb chi, causing it to stagnate. This is why padded cells are effective in sedating people. Slow chi is fine in a bedroom, he says, where the purpose of the room is to invite rest, but bad in offices, where there is work to be done. You can feel stuck, like being trapped in cement.

Nisha takes notes in a leather-bound notebook the size of her palm. It's new, this notebook. It's not her exercise notebook (blue), not her meal-planning notebook (red), and not her awards-and-other-opportunities notebook (yellow). This notebook is green. Lauren doesn't know what green stands for.

When Nisha said she wanted to wait a while longer before deciding whether to renew their lease, in case a better opportunity came along, Lauren thought she meant a better apartment, not a better roommate.

Lauren whispers, "You think I'm stagnating your chi?"

Nisha says, "What? This has nothing to do with you. Shh." A moment later she leans over again. "This is about moving forward in my relationship with Tim."

Lauren says, "You've been dating like two months. How can you know already that moving in together is a good idea?"

Nisha says, "I didn't know you when *we* moved in together."

The university computers randomly spit their names out three years ago, for freshman-year room assignments. Otherwise, they never would have crossed paths. Nisha reminded Lauren of Gina, the new girl who moved to town the summer before junior year of high school. She didn't know anybody when she moved into the house next door to Lauren, so for two months, they were friends, even though Gina had shiny hair and wore expensive jeans and knew everything there was to know about music and fashion. Nisha's areas of expertise are art and design and diet and exercise. There isn't a single subject, no matter how obscure, that Lauren feels confident enough to claim as her own. She doesn't have a disposition that lends itself to connoisseurship, and thus far in life, this has not served her well.

That Nisha and Lauren lived together for nearly three years was a miracle brought about by Nisha's ex-boyfriend Lars. He broke up with her spring semester of freshman year, and Nisha was a wreck. It was the only time Lauren ever saw Nisha lose her balance. Nisha cried for two months straight. Lauren held Nisha in her arms, listened to the same words over and over. She never said, Enough already. She never said, Get over him. She never said, Be strong. Nisha's friends Claudia and Jen said all those things and more. They said, "Bitch, put on something sexy and go get laid."

Not Lauren. She fed Nisha. She did her laundry. And when it was time to finalize living arrangements for sophomore year, Lauren took care of that, too.

College is not the panacea for all the social ills that television shows and movies had led Lauren to believe it would be. Instead, college is like that children's book *Are You My Mother?* Only instead of searching for a mother, Lauren is searching for something more enigmatic. Call it wholeness. Call it composure. Call it serenity. Unlike the baby bird in the story, she has yet to find what she's looking for.

Or more precisely, she's yet to claim it for herself. She knows what it looks like, this inscrutable thing. It looks like Nisha.

Nisha says now, "Anyway, it's been six months. And it's intuition. I feel it."

"It's fast," Lauren says.

"Says the woman who stutters if Geoff Dwyer so much as asks to borrow laundry detergent." Nisha elbows her, then goes back to looking serious, pretending to listen.

Lauren fumbles around Nisha's friends Claudia and Jen as well. They're like a fun house the way they unsettle her, knock her off her feet. When she told Nisha this, Nisha scrunched up her eyes the way she does when they watch scary movies, as though Lauren's life were a gruesome scene she didn't want to watch anymore.

Lauren always knew this day would come, just like she knew it that summer with Gina, but sometimes, she allows herself to hope.

She wonders if the Feng Shui Guru is right, if everything comes down to chi. Nisha's living space mirrors her life: everything is neat and clean and attractive. The same goes for Nisha's appearance. Then there's Lauren: poster corners curling, too many tchotchkes, pants loose where they shouldn't be and tight where they shouldn't be, lip glosses that Nisha says bring out the orange tones in her skin.

The Feng Shui Guru says now that too many mirrors or too much light makes chi ricochet like a pinball. Frantic chi makes people sick, he warns. Especially bad is fluorescent lighting, because the spectrum is distorted, denying the nutrients people require from sunlight and delivering instead a plethora of dis-ease: eye strain, headaches, fatigue, and so forth. He says television has a similar effect. There is even a word for all this: mal-illumination.

The Feng Shui Guru dabs at his forehead with a white handkerchief as though to absorb the toxic photons from the fluorescent lights in the furniture store's ceiling.

*

During the drive back to their apartment, rain falls, and the drops sound like bits of metal clinking against the roof of the car.

The Feng Shui Guru said that chi cycles amongst five basic elements—earth, fire, metal, water, and wood. He talked about the benefits of arranging one's environment so that one element cycles into another: water gives life to wood, wood provides fuel for fire, and so forth. It makes sense until you get to metal chi, which somehow cycles into water chi, but already Lauren can't remember how he explained it—how from metal, you get water. It seems impossible, like Superman squeezing a lump of coal into a diamond. Only substitute a nugget of gold for the coal, and instead of crystallizing, the gold bleeds like a pomegranate.

She can't remember other details, either, like did he say to put your sofa against a wall or no? She wonders, like she does about chemistry and calculus and socializing, if there's a gene for this stuff. You have it or you don't. And if you don't, you're bound for mediocrity at best.

As soon as they enter the apartment, Nisha emerges from her bedroom with cardboard boxes, a pile of newspaper, and a roll of duct tape.

"You're packing already?" Lauren says.

"I'm leaving tonight," Nisha says.

Nisha takes down the silver-framed mirror in their living room. Her reflection says, "Don't worry. I'll still pay my half of the last month's rent."

With the newspaper, she shrouds her reflection, like she's blindfolding it, protecting it from having to look upon Lauren anymore.

Lauren hears the Feng Shui Guru's words: one's surroundings are a reflection of who they are and where they're going.

"Why did you take me to that lecture anyhow?" Lauren says. "You could have gotten out of here several hours earlier."

Nisha stares at Lauren. Calmly she says, "I thought it would be informative. I thought you would learn something. Didn't you learn something?"

Lauren says nothing.

Nisha says, "Well, I thought it was informative." She resumes packing. She wraps the empty wooden frames from the wall, the yellow vase, the candles and their tray.

Soon the living area will be empty except for the television, the only item in the room that belongs to Lauren. Nisha grew up without one. Other than the occasional movie, she can't stand television, likens it to pollution.

Lauren turns it on.

Nisha says nothing, but she packs her dishes and glassware so quickly the pieces clang against each other.

Lauren turns up the volume.

On the screen, a woman waves her arms and screams as she's swallowed by the earth.

Quicksand: but the way the sludge funnels in around the woman's body, the hole in the ground looks like a giant, amorphous vagina. The program cuts to another quicksand scene and then another and another. The narrator says that death by quicksand is the most common television and movie trope of all time.

Soon, two men enter the apartment and carry away the sofa, the coffee table, the dining table and chairs, and Nisha's bedroom furniture. They haul away boxes from Nisha's bedroom that she must have packed days ago.

When the men are done and drive away, Nisha hands Lauren an amethyst-colored glass dome paperweight.

"A token of our friendship," she says.

The paperweight is heavy. Lauren feels as though it's meant to hold her down. Perhaps Nisha finds Lauren's chi frantic, not stagnant. She's trying to tether her, like a dog, keep her from pinballing off the walls and out of the apartment and behind the moving truck.

*

When Nisha closes the door of the apartment behind her, Lauren sits on the floor in front of the television and eats leftover spaghetti from a paper plate and drinks wine from a plastic cup.

On the television, the narrator says characters in quicksand scenes say things like that the key is not to panic, not to flail. Remain calm, and you won't sink any further. But the truth is drowning in quicksand is nearly impossible, because quicksand is about twice as dense as the average human. The more likely dangers are secondary threats that overtake you when your movement is severely impaired: dehydration, predators, sunburn.

When her plate and glass are empty except for the stains the food and wine leave behind, she feels empty too. Around her, the walls are bare. The floor is bare.

The dishes are empty only because she's ingested their contents, of course. She's not really empty. But when she calls the number on the Feng Shui Guru's card, he says that if she feels empty, then she *is* empty. It's the same thing.

"If you feel happy, do you say, I'm not happy; I merely feel happy?" he says.

"No."

Then he says, "You aren't just what you eat. You're that empty plate and glass. You're that table littered with bargain fliers and pleas to donate money to homeless cats. You're that dirty towel on the floor and that raggedy toothbrush in a crusty cup. You're that closet full of ill-fitting clothes. You're that yellowing plant you keep forgetting to water. You're that ugly tchotchke hanging on the wall of your bathroom. You're—"

"Okay, okay. I get it," she says.

She wonders how he sees so much. In the mirror the landlord no doubt put up to make the space appear larger than it is, her shoulders are clenched, her hair limp, her mouth etched with frown lines. Plethora of dis-ease.

She wonders what else people see just from looking at her. The way she knew Nisha was from the opposite end of the spectrum when Nisha walked through the doorway freshman year, everything about her radiant.

Glow

Of a girl the hostess seats at a nearby table with her parents, Cutter says, "That's it, right there. Yesterday she was a girl, and tomorrow she'll be a woman, but today is the day she glows."

I picture a glow stick snapped in two, the barrier between the reactants broken. Neon hues that fade over the course of a day.

Cutter and I are on the clock, behind the bar, but still he squeezes my leg, just above the knee. Wraps his hand around as far as it will go, which is not quite halfway. I recall a detail from one of the *Little House* books I read my niece: the pride Laura Ingalls felt upon learning that when her parents married, her father could encircle the whole of her mother's waist with his two hands.

"She looks like a girl to me," I say. About 13, I guess. Her hair is pulled back into a tight ballerina bun. She can't be much more than a hundred pounds.

"She is, but she isn't," Cutter says. "It's a rare thing to spot in a girl, this moment of transition. Like finding a four-leaf clover."

I look away as though he has opened his mouth to show me what he's chewing.

The restaurant Cutter and I bartend at is in a building that used to be a funeral parlor. Half the restaurant, including the bar, is located underground, where the morgue used to be. The floor and walls are cement, no windows.

Insects and other invertebrates find their way in. Scorpions, centipedes, spiders the width of pint glasses. Once: a mated pair of walking sticks. Right here on the bar, next to the frosted glass vase of citrus fruits.

Cutter didn't see at first that they were a pair. He said, "That thing has two heads!"

I pointed out the two lines, the slightly different shades of brown. The female was longer and triple the male's girth.

"What makes you think that's the female?" Cutter said, and I explained that among insects, and, in fact, most organisms of the animal kingdom, in cases of sexual dimorphism, the female is almost always larger. Because the female often hosts hundreds to thousands of fertilized eggs at once, and those eggs need room to mature.

Now, as the girl in the restaurant lifts her lemonade to her lips and swallows, I think about the eggs in her body and my own. Hundreds of thousands of oocytes clustered together like the clump of subatomic particles in my chemistry textbook's diagram illustrating a radioactive atom.

Decay is a process of slow disintegration. One or a few particles escape the nucleus of a radioactive atom, releasing bursts of energy. Radiation is the rubble. As radium decays, its rubble glows blue-green.

From the two knotty stones that flank a uterus, oocytes break out, one a month. There is rubble there, too.

Cheeks flushed, the girl's skin looks brand new: beautiful, but also vulnerable, like a molted lobster. And glowing? Maybe there is something to what Cutter says.

I lost my virginity on a beach, sand and stubble rubbing my skin raw. Beforehand, the guy talked on and on about philosophy and ancient Greek history while he refilled my plastic red cup with wine from the trunk of his hatchback. He was a junior in college. I was 17 and eager to get on with it. When he placed a hand on my cheek and said, "You're luminous," I laughed, but I'd be lying if I said I didn't want to believe it. Or that when he pushed into me, I didn't fantasize that my gleam was special, that it drew him in like no other light could.

I ask Cutter, "So what happens to this glow you speak of? You're saying it disappears overnight?"

"Not overnight," Cutter says. "Depends on the girl, but it's usually gone by the time she's 20 or 21."

He smiles at me then, says, "Sometimes the glow lasts a little longer."

Cutter is 29. I'm 23, but I can pass for younger. I have a baby face. It runs in my family. My grandmother, who just turned 70, gets mistaken for 60 all the time, she says with pride.

Still, I know I'm decaying. That it's a gradual process that begins with puberty. Each oocyte discarded is a grain of sand slipping through the funnel of an hourglass.

I say, "What about men?"

Cutter laughs, says, "Men are like whiskey. They improve with age."

I want to argue with him, but it's true that I'm attracted to older men. Men who are larger than me, stronger than me, too. My girlfriends and I shrug about this stuff. It's biology. What can you do?

When Cutter and I found that pair of mated walking sticks, I said to him, "She could crush him if she wanted to."

We were alone, setting up, and Cutter pinned me against the bar with the weight of his torso and said, "I suppose she could."

Then I told him that female praying mantises devour their mates. Black widow spiders and orb weavers do it, too. Certain crustaceans and gastropods. I listed the names of various invertebrates like it was foreplay.

Cutter said, "Good thing that among humans, males aren't the weaker sex." He tugged at the skin above my collarbone with his teeth, and I felt heat climb my neck.

Sometimes I pretend to eat my five-year-old niece's foot, enclose her toes with my mouth. She squeals with delight.

Now Cutter squeezes my leg again, and I notice the girl watching us. Cutter notices, too. He winks at her, and she looks away. He grins.

As kids, my sisters and I caught fireflies and smashed their soft bodies against our T-shirts. We ran around making glowing streaks in the dark until the light began to fade. Then we hunted for more fireflies.

But the smaller, weaker, blushing creatures of the world are not always so easily discarded. *P. bucephalum*, a bioluminescent sea slug, slips inside the bell of a jellyfish and slowly devours its host, quickly growing to seven times its original size.

I imagine the jelly is drawn to the slug's glow—so tiny, so shiny and pretty. Like a lantern in the gloom.

I say to Cutter, "Men are like flies, the way they're attracted to radiant things."

The Funny Thing

We're watching Hitchcock's *The Birds*, and you complain about the plot: Birds don't attack for no reason like that.

I say, "What makes you so sure they don't have a reason?"

You squint at me as if you've just woken from a nap and I am a strange room you don't recognize.

Always we hang out at your house because my house is depressing, what with my mother hibernating like a vampire in her dark bedroom. Your mom, on the other hand, buys peach wine coolers and lets us drink them. Your house has all the premium stations and so many pets that there's always something alive to press against.

Only lately you're not so lonely. Every few minutes you glance down at your phone and grin.

The funny thing about you and Ethan Costa: he didn't notice you until Gus Mather burst so many blood vessels in your neck that you took to wearing turtlenecks to conceal the wounds. Those hickeys are like rocket boosters spewing out spent fuel, the way they propelled you, gave you momentum.

The funny thing about you and Gus Mather: he asked me out first, but I thought he wasn't good enough for me.

I didn't understand then that most boys' Number One criterion in selecting a girlfriend is that evidence of her desirability be demonstrated by her first being some other boy's girlfriend.

You take a swig of your peach wine cooler, say Ethan texted that he's coming over later. A blush rises from your green turtleneck: mercury in a thermometer.

I pop a powdered-sugar donut hole into my mouth. Always we suck the powdered sugar off before we eat the cakey centers, but now the sugar tastes chalky and I long to spit the hole out.

"Have you ever thought about how donut holes are named for the empty space their departure leaves in something else?" I say, the hole a hard lump inside my cheek like the balled-up socks we used to stuff inside our training bras during sleepovers.

You ignore me. Punch letters into that phone.

My stepdad Guinotte says all of life is dukkha. Dukkha comes from Sanskrit, literally means to have a poor axle hole. In other words: life is a rickety, ass-bruising ride.

Guinotte says desire is what makes it so. Desire clogs, clutters, makes us sick. Desire is why my mother won't drag herself out of bed—she's filled with the stuff, Guinotte said the other day while stirring pork and beans on the stove. "Filled with—we use that phrasing in conjunction with so many negative emotions: envy, hatred, anger."

"And love," I said.

Guinotte said, "Yes, love is dukkha, too."

To end your suffering, you must empty yourself, he said. Like shaking out the contents of a purse is how I imagine it, only then what good is the purse?

When I told you this, you said, "Your mother's depressed because she's married to an ass who shits on love."

Now your cat's claws draw blood as she kneads my leg, creating a scatterplot of pinpricks, and you say, "I don't know why you let Cleo do that to you."

The funny thing about you and me: I love you more than you love me. I've always been your satellite. Still, when you say, "You don't mind, right? We can watch *Marnie* next weekend," I conjure the shower scene from *Psycho*. The stab, stab, stab of the knife sounded by discordant strings.

Marnie is the second and last film Tippi Hedren made with Alfred Hitchcock. Because she broke her contract. Because Hitchcock tormented her. The key to understanding the plot of *The Birds*: Hitchcock's plot to get his hands on Tippi. He wanted her. She rejected him. So he plotted revenge via hundreds of live birds.

When Tippi's character walks upstairs alone for no discernable reason, despite that birds are jabbing holes in the house's shutters, perforating the wood as easily as paper, you say, "This makes no frigging sense."

"That's what Tippi said," I say.

In Astronomy, Ms. Guttiérrez taught us that contrary to popular belief, stars are not stationary objects around which planets revolve. Stars and planets orbit together around their joint center of mass. Only the greater the discrepancy in their masses, the closer that center of mass is to the more massive object. Thus, most stars appear fixed in space, their only movement their spinning in place. But here's the funny thing: if a planet is close enough to its star and massive enough, the star's revolution around their joint center of mass *is* visible. The planet makes the star tremble.

Hitchcock filmed that iconic attic scene—or bedroom scene, as Hitchcock tellingly referred to it—over the course of five days. Even if the birds' legs hadn't been tied to Tippi's dress with elastics, the birds would have pecked and clawed. They'd been trained to attack.

As Tippi Hedren flails her arms and gasps and moans—if it weren't for the wing flaps, the audio could pass for a sex scene—I wonder aloud how long Hitchcock would have insisted on shooting that scene if it hadn't been for Tippi's nervous breakdown. If her doctor hadn't insisted she be given a week off to recover, that the scene be wrapped up.

"But if he loved her," you say.

There's so much you don't get.

In the ballerina jewelry box I've had since I was a girl, there's half a broken heart dangling from a tarnished chain: "ST NDS." I once complained that you had all the vowels, and you said, "What's so special about vowels?"

As the Rod Taylor character carries the stunned Tippi down the stairs—her eyes vacant, her body limp—I consider what I couldn't quite put to words back then: Vowels are the breath of a word, the beating heart, what gives it life. Until the teeth, tongue, or lips snuff the life out.

The Scream Queen Is Bored

Out on the cabin's porch, the morning after their first night of filming Sequel Number Four. Hot out, only a fitful, feeble breeze like the hopeless breaths of the slain. The scream queen focuses her binoculars on a mangy squirrel scrambling up a pine tree, but then the squirrel disappears, and there's nothing to see.

Frank and the others are drinking coffee in their underwear. Faded boxer shorts, matching bra and panty sets, bed-wrinkled flesh. A cigarette in Frank's lips. Someone suggests a swim in the lake.

Frank says, "Too early," but soon they're running toward the water. Frank doesn't call out to her, but one of the other girls does. "You coming, Carly?"

The scream queen shakes her head. She watches Frank's boxers fall from his pale ass like a raggedy Band-Aid from a wound.

Then there's a series of splashes. Heads bob up, marring the lake's smooth surface. The heads laugh and screech.

If they were filming right now and she were the killer, what would be her strategy? Would she sneak up from below and pull them under one by one? Or play shy, refuse to shed her own clothes upon entering the dark water, a weapon secreted in her pocket? When her first victim screams and blood gurgles to the lake's surface, the others would suspect something bestial, an alligator perhaps. Certainly not the scream queen.

She is always a victim. Because she's female. Because her legs look great in cut-off shorts. Because Frank says that when she opens her throat, every cock within earshot throbs.

Frank is their director. He's also the killer: Victor. Because chasing the scream queen and the other girls, machete in hand, gets him off. Frank isn't ashamed to admit this. The machete is obviously a cock, he says. The girl's screaming mouth is obviously a pussy. He says a monster terrorizing a pretty girl is the oldest fetish there is.

The scream queen used to think Frank was onto something. He'd be pursuing her through brambles, and she'd be running and screaming, and yeah, she'd get hot thinking about what he was going to do to her later in their shared bedroom in the cabin. She'd think words like *ravage* and *plunder*. She'd throb, too.

But lately it all seems kind of pathetic. Ravage and plunder mean to destroy or to ruin, but last night when Frank chased her through the woods with that machete and that grin, she just felt tired. Like anything else you do again and again, running from a psycho killer gets monotonous.

Watching again and again gets old, too, which is why the last sequel didn't get nearly as many views on YouTube.

She told Frank he ought to change things up. "Maybe I could be the killer," she said.

Frank shook his head. "That works in a rape revenge film, but those don't have good sequel potential. And anyway, not really my thing."

"Then at the very least you could swap out the machete for scissors or an axe or, hell, a sharpened pencil."

Frank wouldn't have it, though. He said, "Victor is a machete man."

The scream queen rolled her eyes, but only after Frank turned away. He's a sensitive guy, Frank. Earlier this morning from their cabin bedroom window, heart pounding, the scream queen watched a hawk pluck a rabbit from the earth like a fat tuber. Fifteen minutes later, that rabbit was a bloodied scrap of fluff beneath the hawk's talons. Frank called to her from the shower, "When I get out, I'm going to rip you wide open, Baby. You should see how huge my cock is just thinking about it." She said, "A hawk doesn't need *its* prey to tell it what great big *talons* it has."

The shower ran for several more minutes, but Frank didn't make another sound. She'd taken him by surprise. Slaughtered him so quick, he didn't have a chance to scream.

Tobe's Baby

The baby flipped onto his belly on his descent down the purple water slide, the longest of the five slides in the children's area of the water park. As his face smacked the plastic, his cries stopped. Although it was July, and the water park seemed to have reached maximum capacity, all Loni could hear as she waited for the baby to skid into her arms were the spastic chortles of the baby's father, who grinned at her from the top of the slide.

She'd told Tobe it was a bad idea to send the baby down a water slide. She'd also told him it was a bad idea to smoke weed before going into a water park on a 100-degree day, his eight-month-old baby in tow.

Then, when he'd done it anyway, saying, "Don't tell me what to fucking do, Loni," she'd taken a few hits, too. Wasn't her baby.

A fat cumulous cloud, bulbous as a soggy diaper, smothered the sun just as the baby made his final descent.

Loni caught the baby then, as she imagined a doctor had when the baby had emerged from its mother's vagina.

Loni immediately flipped the baby onto his back against one of her palms and pressed against his sternum with two fingers and blew into his mouth, which was slightly parted, waiting for her breath. She'd taken a CPR-for-infants class with her older sister, Susan, because in her third trimester, Susan was suffering blurred vision and so much nausea she could hardly walk from the sofa to the toilet, much less drive.

Three seconds, five seconds, maybe ten seconds later, Tobe pried the baby from Loni's hands. The look on Tobe's face was a mixture of determination to fix the problem and righteous indignation that he was victim of his good intentions to give the baby some fun. He pumped the baby's chest with the whole meat of his hand, then turned the baby over and slapped its back.

"You're doing it wrong," Loni said.

"Fuck," Tobe said. Then, almost as if to himself, he said, "Heath said you were toxic."

Everything could be toxic if you had too much of it, was what Loni thought. Water, ibuprofen, Vitamin A, sex. Susan said Loni's problem was she fucked the wrong men. But Susan's man couldn't be bothered to take her to CPR class even though her body was about to rupture. The miracle of childbirth. As far as Loni was concerned, pregnancy was cirrhosis of the uterus.

Still, Loni worried for Tobe's baby.

Two pimple-faced teenage lifeguards were distracted by a pig-tailed girl crying out "Mama," over and over again. A third lifeguard poked an older girl in a white bikini in the calf with his toes. A few swimmers seemed to watch Loni and Tobe from behind water-spotted sunglasses.

Later, Loni would wonder 1) why no one responded to their drama and 2) why she didn't call out for help. She'd conclude that 2) she'd been too stoned and 1) only a dumb fuck would get involved with two stoned idiots and a baby.

She said to Tobe, "He needs air," and Tobe was desperate enough to heed her advice. He blew between the baby's parted lips.

A few weeks earlier, Loni had watched the baby for Tobe while he went out with the guys, including Heath, her -ex. She'd danced with the baby to Al Green and Bill Withers, music Tobe and Heath both hated. Then, when the baby had rooted around her chest, she'd lifted her shirt and pulled down her bra, inviting him to suckle.

The baby had switched nipples again and again. Despite repeatedly finding both breasts empty, he'd still believed his circumstances would miraculously change. Loni had laughed at the baby.

Then, as if to punish her, the baby had bit one of her nipples. Chomped down so tight she'd had to pry his lips and then his teeth apart with her fingers. Her nipple had since scabbed and peeled.

She'd felt an impulse to fling the baby against the wall of Tobe's apartment.

But, of course, the baby's anger had been justified. She'd acted as though she had something to offer him.

"Good for you," she'd said to the baby then. "Sticking up for yourself."

She'd retrieved Tobe's ex's breastmilk from the fridge.

Now, as the sun emerged from behind the cloud, the baby finally responded to Tobe's efforts. He cried out. His face reddened as blood delivered oxygen to his cells. Like he was being born all over again.

Watching him, Loni felt as though she was catching her breath, too. She thought then about how even oxygen could be toxic. Oxygen caused cancer. Hence you were supposed to eat antioxidants to prevent cancer. Also, just a little too much oxygen in the air could kill you outright, within minutes. That the percentage of atmospheric oxygen held so steady was more miraculous than egg and sperm making a baby, yet you never heard anybody talk about the miracle of air offering the precise amount of oxygen.

Tobe grinned and said to the baby, "You're okay, you're okay."

The sticky heat coiled around Loni's torso and thighs. Her empty stomach, nothing in it but coffee, felt like a suctioning device. Like her stomach might draw her other organs down into it.

She waded toward the pool's steps and climbed out onto the burning concrete.

Tobe called out to her, "Where are you going?"

She recalled how the pediatrician had treated her childhood peanut allergy by exposing her to minute amounts of peanuts, to help her develop a tolerance to the poison. Eliminating the poison wasn't possible. Peanuts were everywhere.

Of course, tolerance could be toxic, too.

She hoped Tobe was right, that the baby would be okay. Wasn't her problem, though.

I'm Just Talking About Water

It's a Saturday morning and I'm filling a glass with water from the refrigerator when my boyfriend says, "You're supposed to drink water warm or lukewarm, not cold. Your body absorbs it better that way."

When I'm in the shower, he wipes away steam from the mirror and says, "You're supposed to shower in cool water, not hot water. It's better for your skin. Doesn't dry it out."

"So, am I supposed to ignore my instincts? Or always choose what's less pleasurable?" I say.

My boyfriend says, "I'm just talking about water."

*

We're reading the paper and drinking coffee, and he says, "Technically, it's not pedophilia if the girl is fourteen. Adolescents aren't, by definition, children. They're adolescents."

"Absolutely abortion is murder," he says later, handing me a toasted bagel—not toasted enough for my taste, but I don't complain. "Murder is not an age-dependent term."

"So why all this cutting of funding for children's healthcare and other services? Is the point to help ensure those babies grow up to be disadvantaged adolescents who are vulnerable to preying, older white men?" I say.

My boyfriend says, "I'm just talking about language."

*

We're kissing in bed, and my boyfriend puts my hand on his zipper. "Feel how hard I am?" he says.

I mumble, "Yeah."

He says, "Tell me how much you want my big cock."

"I can't say that," I say. "I feel stupid. That's not something I'd of my own volition say. You get that, right?"

My boyfriend sighs and falls back against the bed like a worn-out inflatable punching bag, one that is a little low on air and, therefore, slow to pop back up, and so you're waiting and waiting.

The Point

The shop is one block from the beach—a tourist trap, Eddie calls it. Jill pictures them being yanked off their feet within one of the store's rope net displays, a bearded fisherman in yellow wellies peering down at his catch.

Of course, what Eddie means is there isn't a thing in the store they need. Take the shark's tooth necklaces.

"I've always kind of wanted a shark's tooth necklace," Jill says. The particular tooth that catches her eye is variegated like sandstone.

Upon inspection of the price tag, Eddie says, "For that price, he better have yanked that tooth directly from the shark's mouth with his own two hands." He nods toward the man at the cash register.

Jill says, "I don't see why cruelty increases the value. Anyway, nobody would do that."

"The hell they wouldn't," Eddie says. "There are people walking around in China right now with tiny baby sea turtles swimming inside little pouches of water dangling from their necks."

"How do the turtles survive?" she asks.

A sunburned woman whose dripping swimsuit has left a trail around the store gives Eddie a disapproving look. He eyes her right back as he says, "They don't. They die within a few days."

Although Eddie's grin probably isn't for the sea turtles, Jill wishes his expression were appropriately sober.

When they checked into their motel room earlier, she'd felt so depressed, she'd wished they'd just stayed home.

"There isn't even one pretty thing," she said when Eddie asked what her problem was.

He pulled open the curtain and said, "I bet the sun sets behind that palm tree, too."

Now she says, "What I meant was nobody would pull a shark's tooth because it's stupid dangerous."

Eddie says, "Not if you wear a Kevlar suit. No shark can bite through Kevlar. You'd just need a car jack or something—to pry open the shark's mouth. And a pair of plyers to yank out the tooth. I'd do it. I'd pull a shark's tooth for you, Babe."

Jill says, "I don't want a shark's tooth that way."

A poised woman in a pink sarong and a straw hat points at the glass countertop, where the more expensive jewelry is displayed. The man at the register takes out a long chain with a black pearl pendant. Jill pictures an infinity pool and enormous, fluffy towels.

Too loudly, Eddie says, "Are you going to cry over a kitsch souvenir?"

The woman in the pink sarong gives them a look like you'd give people arguing in a movie theater or during a church service, and Jill says to Eddie then, "Like you'd ever have the money for a Kevlar suit."

Eddie's mouth twists. He's silent for a beat.

Then he says, "That's not the fucking point."

Later, when there are no witnesses, she'll take Eddie's hand and apologize and say, "I have everything I need." And she'll believe she means it.

But now she presses her finger against the tip of the shark's tooth. She thinks about how she's always imagined shark's teeth would be sharp enough to draw blood at the slightest touch, but how this one is disappointingly dull.

Impulses

My friend Elana says, "Research studies have found that mothers who don't work outside the home are no happier than mothers who do."

We're at the playground. It's Saturday afternoon. My kid is throwing handfuls of sand at her kid, which is okay by Elana because she knows her kid has done something to deserve it. Elana's kid has been a bully pretty much since he slid out of her. When our kids weren't even crawling yet and we'd set them down next to each other on a blanket, her kid would pick up the nearest thing he could reach and he'd whack my kid on the head with it. "Sorry. Impulse control issues. That's his Dan half," Elana would say.

Now I say, "But at least those mothers have time to exercise and sleep and eat."

My life is paper towels and Cheerios, and I'm not just talking about my kid. Half the week Cheerios is all I have for lunch at the office. If you think I'm being dramatic, you try working full time and spending every other waking minute wrangling a toddler.

I'm exhausted and bitter as hell, but still, I wouldn't trade any of it to have Luke back, I tell Elana. "That man only ever made things harder."

Elana says, "Same here. About Dan. In the end, at least. I have to say, though, that there was a time when we were pretty darn happy. Like millions of years ago."

I feel as though Elana's just whacked me in the head with a toy block. I picture big, chubby yellow stars swirling around the top of my head like a crown, the way head injuries are depicted in the cartoons my toddler watches. I wonder: why doesn't anyone ever depict these suddenly-visible electric nerve impulses as they really look? Icepicks stabbing black wool, fuzzy puncture wounds of light.

Elana's looking in the direction of the sandbox, only it's more like she's looking through the sandbox and through William and Carolyn and through the trees and even through the Walmart on the other side of the trees, into that distant epoch before we were mothers. I look there, too, and what I see is Luke standing in the rain outside my apartment, a boxed pumpkin pie in his hands. This was when we'd been dating barely a month. He'd decided last minute to ditch his family on Thanksgiving and spend the day with me, knowing I'd be home alone.

Sometimes in those cartoons, there's an initial head injury that makes the character crazy or not themselves somehow, and, curiously, the cure is a second head injury. I remind myself that this rain-drenched, pumpkin-pie-bearing Luke is an example of the first type of injury. He is an errant impulse.

Elana and I are quiet for a while.

Then Elana tells me about another research study she read about: how men who leave their pregnant girlfriends are the unhappiest of all.

Elana should work for one of those tabloid magazines. She's always making shit up.

Before and After

As the pedicurist applies a color called Dancing on Eggshells, the mother-to-be flips magazine pages—before-and-after photos of wardrobe makeovers, weight loss results, and kitchen remodels. She wonders whether the color will show in the photos she eventually frames on the walls of her home. The mother-to-be standing by a lit window, barefoot, her torso draped in gauzy fabric. She will look both earthy and ethereal, like a stone skipping the shimmering surface of a pond, just before the stone sinks.

Only she will not sink: she will shed.

She thinks of the belly-shaped cake her friends presented at her shower—smooth fondant enveloping the crumbly insides like a skin. How the knife sliced through that skin and out came the crumbs and out came the baby, a tiny plastic thing no longer than the tines of a fork. The proportions all wrong, the way the baby, fully formed, took up no more space in the cake belly than a button on a blouse.

The mother-to-be's proportions are wrong, too, which is why she is getting other work done in addition to the removal of the baby. Liposuction in the thighs. A tummy tuck. The sagging bits from her triceps removed. Her doctor warned that she would not be able to hold the baby for several weeks after.

When she emerges from the anesthesia, camera-ready, she will not mind that she cannot hold the baby. She will think of all that she has been unburdened of, and she will feel light, the way she did in college, when she'd stuff pizza and brownies into her mouth and then regurgitate them like a mother bird into the waiting mouth of the toilet bowl. *Before and after*, she'd whisper to herself as she flushed.

Palate Cleanser

See this postcard of a hotel, this window circled in blue ink? That's the room in which I realized I would leave your father. You were there with me, in fact, though I'm sure you don't remember. You couldn't have been more than three. Your father was in Chicago for business, and on a whim, I drove us out of town for the weekend. I'd never done a thing like that in my life. Once we were settled into the hotel, I walked you down the street, a sidewalk shaded by enormous elms, ginkgoes, and maples, to this French restaurant where they served a fixed menu every evening. Three courses, three choices per course. And in between the salad and the dessert: a palate cleanser. In this case, a lemon sorbet served in a little blue goblet. The grin on your face when the waiter set that blue goblet before you! Your own little goblet. For the courses, I had given you bites from my plate. You had eaten that food dutifully, but only the sorbet made you smile—before you even tasted it. Because it was beautiful.

Because it was all yours. That's how I felt at that hotel. It was the first time in my life that I'd stayed at a hotel all by myself. Well, not by myself really. You were there. What I mean is I was the only adult. I was in charge. I could do whatever I wanted whenever I wanted. I could, for instance, take my toddler to a fancy restaurant that her father wouldn't even take me to. It was a feeling I hadn't known I was missing. And once I felt it, I wasn't willing to give it up. Like how after that palate cleanser, when the waiter brought out that one chocolate soufflé for us to share, your grin vanished. Your face reddened. The waiter had barely even taken his hand from the plate. I saw the look of panic on his face. You were the only child in the place, much less the only toddler. It was not the kind of restaurant where one took children. I quickly pushed that soufflé toward you before you wailed.

Eden

While Adam's at work, Eve smears paint samples over the white walls of their bedroom. She tries Love Bite, which in the miniature paint can looks like roses, but on their pale walls makes her think of smashed mosquitoes. She tries Hickey, but it contains too much blue. She tries Smoldering, Flamethrower, and Inferno. Each streak is a lipstick shade. As happens at the cosmetics counter with every crimson hue that looks elegant in its slick tube, she thinks this is the one that's going to change everything. Make her over. Thrust her into the after. But always, she is disappointed. In the rectangular mirror propped on the glass counter, she sees a hopeful smile slaughtered. Adam would say, does say, she's beautiful exactly as she is and that their life together is beautiful. But Eve wants something more. Her name means on the brink, on the verge, on the cusp of something. Perhaps feeling dissatisfied is her fate. She's a child asking, Are we there yet? Adam is the parent saying, Look out the window. Enjoy the view. The view consists of the same green lumps over and over. Only the trees actually change. They're smug with their taut buds blossoming into heavy, red fruit. Nothing ever changes for Eve. Not for lack of trying. She rearranges the furniture every few months, but there are only so many ways to arrange their furniture within this space. She's cycled through the various configurations so many times now that she's built up a kind of tolerance. She'd have to do something truly radical—affix the furniture to the ceiling, say—to feel something. If only her muscles were strong enough, she would. But she can barely push the furniture across the carpet on her own. Staring at those not-quite-reds on their bone-white walls, Eve tries to remember choosing this furniture in a store, choosing this house, choosing Adam. But she can't remember a life before this one. It's as if all these choices were made for her.

Binary Code

The park ranger had been condescending. He wouldn't talk to a group of men that way, the three young women agreed.

They liked running the paved National Park road that cut an eight-mile loop through desert vistas studded thick with wormy saguaros, because it was pretty and hilly and, most importantly, got little traffic. Occasionally a cyclist or two passed, more rarely a car or truck, but otherwise they were alone with what lived there. Lone hawks circling the sky. Lizards scuttling beneath prickly shrubs. Once, as the sun set, they'd spotted a rattlesnake gliding placidly across the road. Another time: a desert tortoise trudging slow as tectonic plates.

And there were many other creatures they couldn't see. That's what the park ranger had warned about. A sign at the park entrance had long cautioned, "Beware of mountain lions," but this morning, the park ranger had told them that yesterday a lone runner had reported being stalked by one of the big cats.

"We're not worried about mountain lions," Nahala had said to the man. With her long, lean legs, Nahala looked like she just might be able to outrun a mountain lion. Until you saw her actually run. Her stride was bouncy, awkward. Chloë joked sometimes that Nahala had a manufacturing defect. "So sleek on the outside, but then you turn her on, and she chokes and sputters."

The park ranger had looked them over, said, "Three of you together, the animal probably won't bother you." But then he turned his attention to the water bottles the women wore around their waists on Velcro belts. "It'll be 95 degrees within the hour probably. People underestimate how much water their bodies lose in this dry heat."

"We've run this loop loads of times," Zade had lied. But the fiction had a ring of truth to it. The point was the women were familiar with this loop, knew the challenges it held in store for them.

They hadn't run it in June before, though. The sun peaking over the mountain as they climbed the first hill felt like yet another judgmental eye on their bodies, its heat intended to antagonize. *Had* they brought enough water? Not that they would turn back now. No way.

Chloë said, "I wonder if there's any scenario in which he would have treated us the same as men. Just waved us in and wished us a nice day. Like maybe if we all dressed like you, Nahala?"

Nahala was the most pragmatic of the three. Ran in the same handful of ratty T-shirts she'd run in since she was fourteen. She gave Chloë shit sometimes about coordinating her overpriced running tops with her hair bands and her socks. Harder to give Zade shit about running in athletic bras and spandex shorts. The desert was hot, after all, and Zade was the serious runner, the one who actually competed in races. Zade could dust the other two if she wanted.

Even as they began their ascent up the steepest, longest climb on the loop, Zade's running voice was hardly distinguishable from her regular voice. "It's not about the clothes. It's about these," she said, placing her hands on her breasts, "and this," moving a hand to the inseam of her shorts.

They were running along the left side of the road, only an ankle-high border of cemented rocks between them and the valley stretching out below. When they reached the summit, they would perhaps pause briefly to take in how far they'd come before continuing on.

Nahala said between ragged breaths, "Being female is like operating with a wonky binary code. We may have infinite choices in how we present ourselves and conduct ourselves, but in the end, men read the same output regardless."

Chloë shook out her arms. "I don't think that's quite right. If a woman comes forward with a rape charge or what have you, she's considered a lot more credible if she dresses conservatively versus sexy."

"Yeah, but either way, she still got raped," Nahala said.

"And either way, you can bet she's going to get a million questions about her drinking and her sex life and why she's trying to ruin that poor man's life," Zade said.

"There's no pattern of dress that can make a woman's autonomy and worth of equal value to a man's," Nahala said.

They were about halfway up the climb, and though they didn't appear to be sweating much, all three felt the grit of salt on their skin. Felt the lightness of the water bottles on their belts.

Just then, a Jeep approached the women from behind, but instead of passing quietly, the driver pressed the horn three times, as if each honk were a mark for a different woman. A chorus of male voices hollered and whistled. The women startled. Their already tired hearts picked up pace. When the jeep passed, they watched the flat silhouettes of naked, big-boobed women bounce and swing with the jeep's mud flaps. Watched the jeep crest the hill and disappear.

As slow as the women were moving up that hill, they knew they'd probably make the same time if they walked. But still, they kept running.

III

III

One or Two?

When the optometrist enters the darkened exam room, he doesn't say a word to me. He slides the door shut. He sits. He breathes. He exudes an odor of wood and earth, as though he's just emerged from the wild, though outside the optometry office is merely a bagel shop, a taco joint, and a mattress store.

Without my contact lenses, I see only his general shape. It's like when a character in a movie wakes from a chloroform-induced unconsciousness: The director shoots the scene out of focus, substitutes sound for sight. An erratic drip. The ticking of a clock. Footsteps echoing against concrete. Neither the viewer nor the character knows yet what's happening, but they're both alert, hearts quickening.

This is what I know: The man in this tiny room, the size of a custodial closet, isn't my usual optometrist. My optometrist asks me how I'm doing. He talks about his children, two boys who both take karate lessons and subsist on a diet of cheese, potatoes, and sugar.

When the optometrist in the room now finally speaks, he says only, "Are you satisfied with your contacts?"

I say, "Uh-huh."

He says, "Excuse me?"

I say, "Yes."

Before a woman in black scrubs told me to wash my hands and remove my contact lenses, the mirror before me reflected a tiny black and white birthday cake on the eyechart behind me. Now I can't see even a smudge of the cake. Being unable to see is like not comprehending the language people are speaking. The optometrist is privy to information I don't have. He could have replaced that birthday cake with an image of two people fucking. How would I know?

The optometrist stands and presses the cold metal of the phoropter, like the name of a dinosaur, against my face. It's an industrial carnival mask. I imagine I look like one of the orgy guests in *Eyes Wide Shut*, only with clothes.

When the optometrist slides a lens—"Better at one or two?"—metal brushes my eyelashes. I worry they'll be guillotined.

I say, "I'm not sure."

He shifts the lens back and forth again.

I say, "The first?"

He says, "Excuse me?"

I say, "One."

We repeat this exchange a few more times. The optometrist leaves the room and returns. I hear the tearing of cardboard, the release of a seal. He turns toward me on his rolling chair and holds out a transparent contact lens on the tip of his finger.

I am nearsighted, not blind. His finger is so close, I can see the grooves of the swirl on his calloused skin. I wonder about what I can't see—bacteria, dirt, a speck of urine or fecal matter or sperm. I read a news article about a guy who killed patient after patient for years on end in terribly botched heart surgeries before officials discovered he'd forged documents, wasn't even a real doctor.

I hear my husband's voice: *Why didn't you just tell him you'd rather not put a contact lens in your eye that has been on someone else's finger?*

A stranger in a movie theater once let his hand slip from the armrest between us and onto my seat. His finger twitched, then grazed my thigh. It happened so slowly I told myself perhaps he was innocent. I was seventeen at the time. He was an older man. Fifty? I thought that perhaps he'd lost the feeling in his fingers. I continued to tell myself this after his finger grazed my thigh again and again.

I'm non-confrontational.

Also, my words would fumble. The optometrist would say, "Excuse me?" and I'd have to start all over again, my mind a warehouse of phoropters clattering back and forth. One or two? One or two?

I take the contact lens from his finger. I put it in my eye.

The optometrist offers me the second contact lens in the same manner.

My eyes tear up. I rub them with the back of my hand. I worry about eye infections. I blink.

Even with blurry vision, I can see there is a box of tissues on the optometrist's desk. But the optometrist just says, "Problem?"

I say, "It itches. I can't see."

Without a word, the optometrist leans in close. I feel the heat of his breath on my cheek. Smell coffee on his lips. I hold my own breath the way I did in the movie theater.

Then, without a word of warning, the optometrist's finger is on my eyeball.

I have the sensation of standing at the edge of a cliff, leaning into the column of air.

The optometrist pulls away, says, "Better?"

I close my eyes. I'm ashamed to look at him. But once again, I'm uncertain about what's happened. I don't fault my dentist for putting his hands in my mouth or my gynecologist for swabbing my cervix.

Then again, this is not my optometrist. How do I know he's not some pervert who gets off on touching people's eyeballs?

No one, not even my husband, has ever touched my eyeballs.

I think about the other parts of me no one has touched—my bones, the bundle of nerves encased in my spine, my heart.

That heart surgeon imposter, there must have been details his patients chose to overlook: Misused medical terms? A wildness in his eyes?

As the anesthesiologist put the mask to their faces, did they wonder, not for the first time, if the man about to dig into their chests and unearth their glistening, defenseless hearts wasn't in the business of healing? Maybe they felt a strange thrill at the idea that the man wanted only to put his hands where no one else had been. Maybe they welcomed the grogginess of the anesthesia, the way it quieted the mind's clattering.

Business Enough

In college, I took a psychology course in which I learned about serotonin and dopamine and Phineas Gage. I've forgotten the mechanics of serotonin and dopamine, but I think often of Phineas Gage, the man who survived an iron rod shooting through his skull. It happened on the job, while he blasted away rock to clear the way for railway tracks. A chance spark set the dynamite off prematurely. Story has it he was unconscious only for a moment, then stood and rode an oxcart back to town, where he famously said to the local doctor, "Here is business enough for you." Later, as the doctor peeled dried bits of brain from Gage's scalp and plucked shards of bone from the wound, Gage spat out brain tissue and blood that drained into his throat.

Phineas Gage is who I think of when my supervisor reminds me that, with fewer than fifty employees, the company isn't required to grant me maternity leave. And when, between breast milk-pumping sessions, my blouse stained and my fingers cramping, I fill out daily reports, weekly reports, quarterly reports, and annual reports concerning what I have contributed to the company. And when a dear friend dies from mesothelioma, a death tracing fifty-plus years back to when she played with asbestos her mother shook from her father's work clothes when she washed the family's laundry.

Phineas Gage lived twelve years with that hole in his head. Dismissed from his railroad job because he was no longer considered suitable, he went on to become a stagecoach driver, as well as the most renowned neuroscience case of all time. Now his skull and the tamping iron that made it legendary are on display at the Harvard Medical School. But I'm not convinced Gage's case was so extraordinary. What he had on the rest of us was simply a matter of showmanship.

Snapshot

She was driving home, the mountains starting to purple like turnip tops, when she saw a man with his head in his hands. He was in his car, which was parked off the road in the field of dirt in front of that new church, the one with the sign that read, "Too Cold to Change Sign. Sin Bad. Jesus Good. Details Inside." She glimpsed the man briefly, for she was driving, and there was no red light, no red sign telling her it was okay to stop. She glimpsed him briefly, yet she saw so much, too much. She tried to explain to her husband later how that man's anguish had affected her. She told him how she'd pictured herself pulling over, knocking on the man's window, saying something to comfort him, something like "I see you," but how then she thought, but what if he's a misogynist? What if he's violent? She said, "That's what it is to be a woman in this world. You can't even empathize with a stranger without thinking about your own safety." Her husband just said, "Probably he wasn't a misogynist." She didn't bother then to tell him the other thing she saw on her drive—that someone had wrapped that metal horse sculpture in a blanket. Some feelings were difficult to explain, like last week when her son had peeked underneath the unsealed flaps of the brown cardboard box sitting next to her desk as she'd paid the overdue water bill. He'd said, "What's in here?" She'd snapped her head. "Don't look in there!" But it had been too late. In those milliseconds, he'd seen the birthday gift she'd planned to wrap after she paid the water company. She told her son he shouldn't assume that's what he'd get. She might decide to exchange the gift now that he'd seen it. His birthday was a week away, after all. But all week she sensed that he knew she wouldn't exchange the gift—it was what he'd asked for, after all—and that he was burdened by this knowledge. The morning of his birthday, when he tore open the big blue package, far larger than the gift warranted, he smiled wistfully. "It's just what I wanted," he said, but they both knew that was only partly true. Her husband snapped their photo, beamed as though everything were perfect.

Deposition

Midnight, and Sam is burying the spoons again. Because he thinks burying the spoons is the trick to getting me pregnant.

"Why spoons?" I asked the first time he did it. It's not just the delicate silver teaspoons that he buries, the spoons we inherited from his mother and that look like they might actually hold some magic. He buries every spoon in our kitchen. The plump soup spoons that are too wide for a small child's mouth. The sweet little clay spoons I made in pottery classes back when I still took pottery classes. The soft wooden cooking spoons, too.

"Spoons are sensual," Sam said.

"I guess," I said, but I knew what he meant. I used to think when I was shaping them out of clay about how the curved scoop of the spoons felt like breasts, the handles like weirdly slender penises. Like a cat penis maybe, only longer.

They're a fertility symbol if there ever was one.

After Sam buries the spoons, we have sex. Is the sex good? Sometimes it is. Sometimes I'm so tired I practically sleep right through it. Other times I can't relax. Can't stop picturing him burying those spoons. His fingers digging in the dirt. The way sweat beads on his forehead.

Sometimes he sounds like a raccoon scurrying around in the moonlight. That past February raccoons plucked the fruit I'd left on our orange tree. They peeled those oranges as neatly as any human. The rinds scattered beneath the tree made me think of shed exoskeletons.

Every morning just before sunrise Sam digs those spoons up again. Because that's part of the ritual. The spoons must be unearthed before light touches the soil, or the trick won't work.

How long has he been doing this? Eleven weeks now? Seventeen? I don't know anymore.

I know this: the only thing that's changed shape around here is the spoons. Every day they look a little more worn, a little more bent. And every day they make the food in our mouths taste a little bit more like dirt.

Night Bloom

Rachel has been deflecting Kat for months, but then she invites Kat to her apartment to swim. It's a strange invitation: Swim? The kind of thing Kat did with girlfriends when she was a teenager. Around Rachel, she feels like a teenager, despite being forty-six to Rachel's thirty. Right now, standing in Rachel's living room, Kat's underarms are so wet, sweat is dripping down her torso like condensation along the glass panes of a greenhouse. Because (surprise!) Emer, a member of Rachel's chemistry coterie, is here. Chemistry grad students might not immediately come to mind when one thinks of prickly, cliquish types, but Rachel introduced Kat to Emer and the rest at a tapas restaurant, and as Kat cut into her pulpo gallego—octopus braised in paprika—every one of those women looked at her as though she were a corpse flower emanating its scent of rotting flesh.

When Rachel lets Kat into the apartment—"Kat, you made it!" as though Kat had not texted Rachel that she was coming—Emer doesn't acknowledge Kat. This despite that the sliding glass door to the balcony is open, and Kat can easily detect Emer's jasmine perfume, mingled with Rachel's gardenia scent. Always flowers. Emer's standing out there in a green bikini, her fingernails and toenails painted a pale pink. She holds up a can of sunscreen and sprays herself, and, collaterally, the potted plants Kat helped Rachel pick out and arrange. The chemical blend is nauseating. Kat worries about the goldenrod in the large blue pot. It's particularly sensitive to pollutants.

False advertising is typical of Rachel. Once she tried to set Kat up with one of her chemistry professors, whom she sold as artsy and "fiendishly good-looking." Kat only agreed to the date because she was curious to see what Rachel considered a "perfect match" for her. Turned out the "art" this guy was into was Japanese comics depicting childish-looking women with boobs the size of Thanksgiving hams. He whipped a stack of them out of his messenger bag, right there at the bar. By fiendish, she'd meant he had a devilish beard. By perfect match, Kat gathered that Rachel meant he was fiftyish, his hair graying like Kat's.

When Rachel tried to set Kat up again, the second time with a woman, from Rachel's gym, Kat declined. What would she have in common with someone who ran six-plus miles a day on a treadmill?

If Rachel had told Kat she was inviting anyone else to swim, Kat wouldn't have said yes. Rachel's other friends are the reason Rachel has been avoiding Kat. Or more aptly, Kat expressing her opinion that Rachel is too interesting to be hanging out with such boring people is why. She pinpointed John specifically—John who is now smiling at her from five photographs displayed on Rachel's bookcase. Kat said he was immature, which he is. He's twenty-five and spends his free time playing shoot-'em-up video games. Then Kat likened him to a dandelion puff. That she compared Rachel to an orchid did not nullify the dandelion comment.

In Kat's defense, Rachel once said she appreciated Kat's honesty. She'd emerged from her closet in an orange halter dress that Kat said made her look jaundiced, and Rachel said, "Damnit! I was worried about that. Why did Emer let me buy it?"

Because Emer is like *Arisaema griffithii*, a lily with the head, and tongue, of a cobra.

At the pool, Rachel and Emer arrange their towels on chaise lounges. Then they arrange their bodies, so their swimsuits expose only the flesh they want exposed. Kat thinks of window displays.

Rachel is wearing a bikini, too—hers a blue-gray that matches her eyes.

Kat lies on the chair on the other side of Rachel. She keeps her cover-up on but reluctantly allows the sun to shine on her legs even though she frets about sun damage no matter how high the SPF of her sunscreen.

"So, what's been up with you?" Rachel says to Kat.

When Rachel sent the invitation by text earlier in the day, she asked the same question, and Kat texted back an itemized summary of the previous five months: *March—visited my mother in the hospital (gallbladder surgery); April—joined a meditation group, got rid of my television and cable; May—broke a toe, joined a feminist reading group; June—went to Arizona to see the Queen of the Night in bloom; July—acquired a new orchid, submitted my doctoral dissertation.*

So now Kat says, "I told you already."

"Oh, right," Rachel says. "You finished your dissertation. You must feel accomplished."

"I do," Kat says.

To Emer, Rachel says, "Kat studies night-blooming flowers—plants that bloom for only a few nights and then they die."

"I study the relationship between the flowers and their pollinators. And not all night-bloomers bloom so briefly. You're confusing the life of an individual flower with the blooming season of the plant," Kat says. She's told Rachel all this plenty of times, including the night they met. They'd both gone to view the university's collection of Nottingham catchflies in bloom; or, more precisely, Kat had gone to view them, Rachel to smell them. A heady, sweet scent like hyacinth. Rachel had been the strange woman who had pitched a fleece blanket beneath one of the blooms. She was lying there with her eyes closed, not even looking at the flower. When she did open her eyes, it was to reach her finger up and touch the pale green stigmas. Kat's first words to her had been, "You're a strange breed of pollinator."

Emer says, "Right. Evening primrose blooms for months."

They are alone at the pool and hermit-prone Kat is surprised to find herself longing for kids to come out and make some noise splashing around the pool. The quiet makes her feel conspicuous, like that tentacled pulpo gallego flanked by Rachel's other friends' more discreet plates of croquettes and empanadas.

She says to Rachel, "So, you and John are doing well, I take it. I noticed the photos."

Emer is the one who responds. "They're engaged. Didn't you notice the ring?"

Kat never notices rings, a blind spot that has gotten her in trouble a few times. But she looks now, and sure enough, Rachel's left hand is adorned with a diamond on a white gold band.

Kat doesn't mention that Rachel once said there was no way in hell she'd ever wear a diamond. Not even an ethically sourced diamond because diamonds "are so generic." Rachel's words.

"Well, congratulations," Kat says.

"Well, thanks," Rachel says.

Emer says, "He wrote out his proposal in element symbols. Tungsten-iodine-lutetium-argon-yttrium-neon."

Kat says, "Will you ary ne?"

Rachel says, "He made a few edits. Wrote in the two m's, subtracted the n. It was sweet."

What Kat thinks: she should have known that *Want to come over to swim?* meant something other than swim.

And she should have been more specific when she compared Rachel to an orchid, selected a species known for its trickery, like The Laughing Bumble Bee orchid, *Ophrys Bomybliflora*. The flower looks so much like a bumblebee that real bumblebees try to mate with it. Like how Rachel fooled Kat once by kissing her at a bar. Some guy—the now-fiancé John, in fact—said to them, "Are you two together-together?" They were just drinking martinis and talking, but maybe he could see what Rachel seemed not to grasp. In response, Rachel leaned in and put her lips to Kat's. Kat swore later to her friend Joanna that the kiss was hella convincing, except that when Rachel pulled away, she winked at John.

Or maybe the type of flower is inconsequential, because all flowers are tricksters. Their raison d'être is to seduce, to manipulate. Even dandelion puffs. What child hasn't put her lips to one and blown?

Joanna said, "Straight female friendships have all the drama of romantic relationships, only minus the perk of sex."

Then she said, "Still, your problem is you're always rounding up."

Kat said, "But *she* kissed *me*."

Joanna said, "Round down and you get this: She used you as a prop."

That kiss had been as heady as the scent of the Nottingham catchfly. It couldn't have simply been a performance, Kat had told herself.

But nothing more happened. It was a one-night event. Like the night-blooming cereus she'd gone to see in bloom that June.

Kat had planned to sit with the flower for several hours, but all the cellphone camera flashes had ruined her enjoyment. She supposed she should be impressed so many people cared about visiting a botanical garden at night just to see a rare bloom, but the way they circled the plant with their phones in front of their faces, contorting themselves to capture different angles, depressed her. She'd barely lasted twenty minutes before returning to her hotel room and ordering a pizza. Of this, Joanna said, "You imagined people would just stand there quietly and appreciate the flowers? Round down, woman. Round down."

In fact, Kat's thinking had been even more ridiculous: she'd imagined she'd find a cereus nobody else had found and so she'd have the plant all to herself.

Kat says to Rachel now, "I'm going for a swim."

Rachel says, "Let us know how the water is," even though Kat knows that nothing she might say would inspire Rachel to leave Emer's side to join Kat in the chlorinated, pee-filled pool.

Kat stands. She pulls off her cover-up. Just a month ago, she would have kept the cover-up on, only dipped her toes. But she decides that at forty-six, she is too mature to worry about what a couple of thirty-year-old women think of her body. Let them think of themselves as flowers all they want. As she has had to remind Rachel, while plants may bloom for months on end, individual flowers are short-lived organs. Sometimes they get replaced, sometimes they don't, but soon enough, they all wilt.

Dead Plant

"Does it count as out of place if it's dead?" I say to Jeff.

He's taken cleaning house to a whole new level recently, ever since my mother's Alzheimer's got worse and we had to fly out to Texas to help her and my stepdad clean up their house and put it on the market. That house was a disaster in every way. Nails sprouting up out of the floorboards like steely, stray hairs. The fruit bowl coated in a silvery green mold. Mail dating back to three years ago still piled on the dining room table. Cockroaches watching us from every crevice. Jeff was appalled, but, also, he was amazing. He took a deep breath and he got to work. Directed me gently, like a preschool teacher wrapping a child's hand around a pencil for the first time.

Now that we're back in our own house, Jeff's big thing is everything should have a designated place and if it doesn't, there's a good chance we don't need it.

I told him everything in my office is where it belongs. Then he came in and pointed to the half-knitted scarf draped over everyone from Ellison to Eugenides, the tin of thumbtacks blocking his face in our wedding photo, the plant.

"Dead is worse." He shakes his head. "You can't keep anything alive."

"That's simply false," I say. "I've been alive forty-six years, haven't I?"

"Your parents get some credit for the first eighteen. I get some credit for the last eighteen," he says.

I can't argue with him about the last eighteen. Jeff has probably saved me from myself more times than I can count. But as for the first eighteen, Jeff knows full well I'd reduce that figure to about two. I was raised by the microwave more than the pair of humans who begat me.

Jeff says, "How long has it been dead? Days? Weeks?"

I pause before answering. The truth is I'm not sure that plant was ever alive in my office. Seems like it was a matter of hours after I brought it home from the nursery that it began to lean over. Leaning towards the window, towards the sun, I told myself. Plants will bend in all kinds of crazy ways to reach what they need. Hard to reach water, though, when it's down the hall; second door on the left. It was a matter of days before that plant shriveled and its sage green leaves browned and crinkled.

"Years," I say.

Jeff's eyes widen. "Why would you keep a dead plant around for years?"

It's a good question I don't have a good answer to.

"Because it makes me sad to admit it's dead?" I say.

This does make me sad. I have a vision of my house being full of thriving things. I go to the plant nursery on my lunch hour sometimes. I spend the whole hour stroking stems, breathing in that fortifying smell of damp earth, thinking about how this time I'm going to keep the plant I buy alive.

But I'm bad at follow-through. That half-knitted scarf: I started it three years ago, a birthday gift for my friend Katrina.

"How many plants is this now? Twenty? Forty?" Jeff says.

"Don't be cruel," I say.

I don't know why I don't follow through on simple things like giving a plant water or disposing of said plant after it's dead. It's not that I forget exactly, more that I seem to surrender to things falling apart. Or maybe *surrender* isn't the right word exactly. My shoelace starts to fray, and I pull at the threads. Help the lace along in its unraveling. It's a genetic trait, I tell myself, or an instinct, something innate that is almost impossible to resist. Like a pig rolling around in the mud, making that mud pit wider and deeper with every twist. I remember how my father winced at what our two pigs did to his land. He bought those pigs when I was nine, around the same time he bought the goats and the turkeys and took up black-smithing. His maker phase. He didn't anticipate how much destruction his making would entail.

Jeff says, "How much longer would you have kept this dead plant around?"

"Honestly?" I say. "Maybe forever."

Just like if it hadn't been for my stepdad crying into the telephone, I don't know that I ever would have gone out there to see my mother.

Carrot

When Helen Cuddy was a girl, she once yanked a massive carrot from a grassy field in a public park. She'd thought she was ridding the park of a weed. When the orange bulge emerged from the earth, she couldn't have been happier than if that carrot had been made of gold. A carrot! To think that countless children had passed by the inconspicuous clump of green, giving it no thought at all. Years later, she joked at a party that her gravestone ought to read, "Here lies Helen Cuddy. She found a carrot! Growing all by its lonesome in a public park!" Her partner J.T. then said, "Or maybe it should read, 'Here lies Helen Cuddy. She found a carrot once. She was on the lookout for stray carrots forever after, but she never did find another one.'"

Snow White with Goats

The house got held up in traffic, she said, which is why she and the goats had made camp in the little park across the street from our houses. She unrolled a patchwork blanket by the playground our children had outgrown.

Of course, there was no house. There was no doubt in our minds of that. Only a lunatic would travel with goats as her companions. Only the homeless would take up residence on a playground.

But such a pretty lunatic, we couldn't help watching her through slats of shutters, at the thick edges of curtains while our husbands were away at work. Watch her stroke those goats' coarse heads with her slender hands. Watch how she laughed when the goats nibbled at the hem of her dress.

Only the shiny metal slide on that playground was functional. It must be coated in something to have lasted this long in our tropical climate. The monkey bars had long since rusted. The wooden seesaw had grown mossy and slippery. The slide, though, it was grand. The goats loved it.

They loved her, too.

Who wouldn't? That sweet, vanilla smile. Those dark curls and quaint white cap. That buttery skin. Red pumps not leaving her feet even when she lay down on that blanket to take a nap beneath the tree with the brittle tire swing. She could make even a swamp place like this seem homey.

We took to calling her Snow White.

Our husbands, who didn't notice anything, noticed her, too. They said, it's so hot out. They said, if she says her house is being delivered, maybe it is. They said, maybe we should invite her over for dinner? Is there enough for three?

There is not enough for three, we said.

But by the fourth day, the mercury had risen above one hundred, the air was syrup, and she and the goats drooped like wet laundry from a line. Should we call an authority? We wondered. Gilda, who lived in the egg yolk-colored house with the irises that sprung up every April, pointed out that the park was public property. Technically, the young woman was in her rights to be there. The goats: maybe not so much. But they weren't hurting anyone, and they trimmed the weeds, so we let them be. We offered bottles of water, umbrellas for shade.

We didn't offer our spare bedrooms to her, though, when she eyed our houses as we handed over that water. She probably wouldn't have accepted such an invitation anyway if it didn't extend to the goats, we reasoned. Also, she was a stranger. Also, she was a lunatic. Also, and most importantly, she was too beautiful. We understood why the queen/stepmother in that story wouldn't want the girl too close, why she wouldn't want Snow White in her home.

We didn't think we understood the murder part, the order the queen gave to the huntsman to bring her Snow White's heart; or the spell part, bewitching the girl to an eternal sleep. But by the fifth afternoon, when the young woman hadn't risen all day, hadn't moved as far as we could tell, we shuddered momentarily at our relief.

We did what any good neighbor would do—put out water for the goats, let them mow our lawns.

Then, on the evening of the seventh day, would you believe it? A house did arrive. Two massive flatbed trucks unloaded the wooden structure next to the slide. Nobody ever did un-board the windows.

Cake or Pie

Rhoda's husband, Don, says maybe he should put out an ad seeking a partner better suited to life in the end of days.

This is after he comes home with a trunk full of dry beans and rice, and after Rhoda says she would wither and die on a diet of dry beans and rice. "What about butter? And flour and sugar and eggs? If I'm going to hunker down and hide, I need pastries. I need coffee and wine. Otherwise, what's the incentive to staying alive?" And after Don says, "The incentive is survival. Also, what if the power goes out? That butter will become rancid. The oven will be useless." And after Rhoda says, "But what if the power doesn't go out and we suffer needlessly?" And after Don gives her an exasperated look and says, "There's no baking in doomsday prepping."

Rhoda's problem, according to Don, is she's governed by appetite, and appetite is fickle. She's unpredictable even to herself. They'll go out to their favorite Italian restaurant because Rhoda wants ravioli, but once there, she'll deliberate for fifteen minutes over the veal marsala, the chicken saltimbocca, and whatever special the waiter describes with what Don considers to be overly precious words.

As Don stacks the dry beans and rice next to his other stores—hefty bags of oats, a vat of peanut butter, stacked boxes of saltine crackers—he says to Rhoda, "You want too much."

Rhoda considers all that Don wants.

She envisions Don scrutinizing prospective end-of-days partners' resumes for inconsistencies. "Says here you're detail-oriented, yet the next line is missing a period and 'responsible' is spelled with an 'a.'"

She pictures him sitting across from these women and gauging how matter-of-factly they look him in the eye when answering his questions, whether they fidget their hands, tug at the waists of their jeans to tuck in bits of belly that would otherwise poof out like pillows from clumsily made beds.

He will be looking for someone without impulses to restrain or hide.

But also, someone who would be good at hiding when the world comes to that, as Don believes it will. Someone who can keep still and keep her mouth shut whole days. Someone whose desires are discreet. Someone easily satisfied. Or maybe: someone for whom satisfaction is not necessary, for whom survival is enough.

Rhoda imagines his first interview question will be "Cake or pie?" If the candidate says "cake" or "pie," she's out. Because the right answer is neither. The right answer is that sugar has no nutritional value. The right answer is sweetness is nonessential.

But Rhoda thinks the look on Don's face as he talks about what he still needs to purchase for their pantry and what he needs in a partner in these times resembles that of a child anticipating the tinkling music of an ice-cream truck. One who doesn't speak the language of doomsday prep might think "frugality" and "practicality" and "going without" mean "compote" and "cream" and "toasted meringue."

Frogs in Captivity

Over dinner, I say, "Where do you think fire forms in a dragon? Its belly? Its lungs? Its mouth?"

You say, "I've had a rough day," and fork carrots and potatoes into your mouth.

I say, "It's an intimate thing to talk to a person face-to-face, your noses uncovered. You breathe each other in. Not just perfume or deodorant, or the coffee you've been drinking, but shed skin cells."

I say, "I wish we spent more time together."

You say, "I'm exhausted."

I say, "I read that if you want to breed frogs in captivity, you should play them audio of a thunderstorm."

You say, "I think I might be getting sick."

I say, "Seriously, this dragon question: What do you think the combustion reaction is that enables a dragon to breathe fire? What elements or compounds do you think are involved?"

You say, "I can't deal with getting sick right now."

I say, "I feel like you don't listen to me."

You say, "Hydrogen and oxygen can be explosive."

I say, "And oxygen feeds a fire. Seal a lit candle from oxygen by covering it with glass, and the flame burns out."

You say, "My hearing's bad."

I say, "Then get a hearing aid."

You say, "Let's just say I don't listen to you."

I say, "Dust is residue of bodies—human bodies, dust mite bodies, the decayed matter of still other bodies. Then there are the dust mites themselves, the living feeding off the dead."

You say, "I'm spending time with you right now. Are you going to finish that chicken?"

I say, "Maybe the dichotomy of living and nonliving misses the point. What is living today was once nonliving and will be nonliving again. What is nonliving was likely once living and will be living again."

You say, "I hope you're not going to become a vegetarian again."

I say, "You never ask me how my day was."

You say, "One doesn't want to risk harm."

I say, "I bet exhaling fire is a torment."

You say, "You can say that again."

I say, "I get tired of repeating myself."

My Husband Is Always Losing Things

While my husband frantically searches the house for his misplaced eyeglasses, I watch Marie Kondo fold socks, then stockings, then a sweater into neat little rectangles. They look like origami handbags. In her signature white jacket, the Japanese tidying expert instructs viewers to stroke each garment. She says, "Send the clothing love through your palms." She runs her hands gently down both the sleeves and the body of a fluffy white sweater, and my skin tingles.

My husband passes through the living room for the fifth time this search. He says, "You sure you didn't move them?"

Sometimes he'll point to an empty spot on a counter and say, "I know I left it right there." "Then why isn't it there?" I'll say. Sometimes he'll say, "Because you moved it." Other times, "Because you took it." Then I'll say, "Why do you think I took it?" He never has an answer for that.

Once I said, "Then come take it back." I was standing in the doorway to his home office in a dress I hadn't worn in years, a dress I'd decided to make myself wear, even if only to lounge about the house, because I had read that it's a mistake to save our favorite clothing for special occasions that never arrive. I imagined him frisking me for the lost object, like a TSA agent searching for contraband. But my husband didn't look up, kept shuffling around papers, emptying out boxes.

I used to find his tendency to lose things amusing; then I found it irritating; now it mostly makes me sad. Like when he lost the rack of lamb I asked him to pick up from the butcher, and I found the five pounds of muscle and bone sweating on the floorboard of the passenger side of the car. He couldn't blame me for that one. After putting the lamb in a plastic trash bag and dropping it into the garbage, he said, "Don't look at me like that. It was an accident. You want me to go out and pick up another?" "No," I said. I'd lost my appetite.

To get your house in order, the first thing to do is to discard, Kondo says. Take every object into your hands and ask, "Does this spark joy?"

I stiffen at these words. It's a harsh test, isn't it? Joy isn't the only measure of value.

Take wood chips, for example. For years, they've accumulated on the floor of our garage at the rate of dog hair. But when my husband sprinkled them over the puddle of oil that leaked from the car, and they soaked up the mess, left no stain, I was half-grateful he'd not cleaned the garage in twenty years.

Kondo says this is why stroking and folding clothing is important. It isn't only a matter of caring for your things. Touch allows you to assess how you truly feel about each item.

I call out to my husband, "They're not already on your face?" I am not joking. He has ransacked the house for objects that were already on his person—in his pocket, around his neck, in his hand.

Kondo demonstrates with two sweaters. She caresses the first sweater, smiles, places it down beside her. She caresses the second sweater, and the cool look on her face says the item does not pass inspection. I think of the scoliosis screenings at school when I was a kid, how every time a PE teacher told me to bend at the waist so she could scrutinize my spine, I tensed up, certain the test would reveal some defection.

Kondo doesn't offer a word about why the second sweater doesn't pass the test. She says to listen to your intuition when deciding what to discard. Rationalization deceives. You rationalize that discarding an object is wasteful or that you might need it again someday. Of the second sweater, she says, "I want to thank this for keeping me warm, but now it's time to let it go." She places the sweater apart from the sweater she's keeping. She smiles again, her expression serene.

After discarding, the next step is to assign a home to each object you keep. Value what cannot be seen on the outside, Kondo says, meaning the insides of closets, cabinets, and drawers. What is hidden from public view is all the more sacred.

I think about how my friend Sara worried when her doctor scheduled her for an MRI to diagnose the source of her back pain. Not just because of the invasiveness of the procedure or concern for what the doctor might find. Sara worried there might be metal inside her that she didn't know about. "How can I be sure there isn't?" she said. What could I possibly say to assure her? The body is an unopened drawer.

Except when it *is* opened, by surgeons, and you are out cold as they root around inside you. Or when MRI technicians or X-ray technicians or TSA agents scan your insides—yet another piece of luggage.

Sometimes I wish I could see inside my husband. Peel back the skin and muscle, cut through the bone. Reveal the hidden spaces. Only the clutter might be worse than I imagine. I fear what I might find there, or not find. Would I be able to locate myself at all?

Return

I was sitting in my car, waiting for the mall to open, when a woman I no longer wanted to be friends with knocked on my window. It was a hundred degrees out already, though it wasn't quite ten in the morning. My car's air-conditioning was set to maximum. Plus, there was the matter of my no longer liking her. I was reluctant to put the window down.

"What took you so long?" she said when I finally pressed the button.

"I didn't want to let the cool air out," I said. "Also, I don't want to be friends with you anymore, as you know."

She blinked at me. "We've been friends for twelve years. I took you to the hospital when you fell and hit your head. I picked your children up from school that time when you could not. I was there for you when you divorced your husband." She said all this matter-of-factly, as though these actions disputed any claim I could possibly make against her.

Then she eyed the shopping bag on my passenger seat. "You have a return?"

"That's right," I said.

"I'll go with you," she said. "I was heading to that store myself."

When one of the saleswomen unlocked the doors to the store, I went straight to the customer service desk. The woman I no longer wanted to be friends with followed.

The saleswoman behind the counter said, "You have a return?"

"I do," I said, and I removed the duvet and pillow shams from the shopping bag and placed them on the counter.

The saleswoman said, "Anything wrong with them?"

"I just changed my mind," I said. And then because I have a habit of justifying returns, as though the saleswoman will judge me, think that I damaged the item or that I bought something I cannot afford, I added, "I thought they would look good in my bedroom, but they do not. The colors don't complement the paint on my walls."

The saleswoman said, "Sure. No problem." She scanned my receipt and refunded the sum back to my credit card. The entire process took less than two minutes.

I said to the woman I no longer wanted to be friends with, "See how easy it was to return something simply because I didn't want it anymore?"

She said, "Had you slept on that bedding?"

"No," I said.

"Had you run it through the washing machine?"

"No."

"Had you spilled wine or coffee on it?"

"No."

"Your cat barf on it?"

"No."

"How long had you had it?" she asked.

"One week," I said.

"Well, there you go."

No Knees

Worse things can happen than spotting your ex strolling through the park with a robot. Not a sleek automaton, mind you, but a creature so primitive it squeaks with every step.

"Can a robot be primitive?" the current says. "Isn't synthetic sort of the opposite of primitive?"

We're walking hand in hand and so are my ex and that robot that looks like a kitchen-sink salad of random parts. The robot's head is, I'm pretty certain, the pot my ex and I used to make soup in. Its shoulders the fat, coily metal piping that connects the back of the washer and dryer to the wall. I don't know the terms for these things. My ex used to tease me about my ignorance of all things mechanical. My current and I just call up her cousin Ned when water oversteps its boundaries or when the screw that holds everything together comes loose.

A few years ago, I would have said, did say, that my ex can take everything, do what she wants with it. I didn't care, I said. In fact, I said I'd be happier with nothing. That's how much she drove me crazy. Didn't get me at all.

My ex's reply: she would, in fact, take everything and with it she'd make something better than she ever had with me.

Now the fiery pink of sunset is fading, and the gloom is settling in its place—squashing the fiery pink really, like the current's cat does my hands when I'm trying to type.

"You mean the gloaming," the current says.

The current knows what I'm thinking before I say it. There was a time when the newness of this was sparkly and exciting. Like my ex's robot, I guess, before you see it try to take a step from the hip.

Common Denominator

I haven't seen my mother in twelve years. That's what I tell Dale's sister when she says, "Didn't your mother ever tell you not to date men who don't know how to cook?" and after Dale says, "But I know how to wash dishes."

Tanya's eyes widen. "Twelve years?"

The three of us are in Dale's kitchen, drinking wine and chopping. Rather, Tanya and I are chopping. Dale hates cooking, it's true. He hovers outside the action, useless, like me at my kid's Boy Scout outings. The other parents teach the kids about finding shelter in the woods, tracking animals, and stabbing sticks into marshmallows, while I hide out in my tent, inspecting every surface for ticks.

I've been dating Dale about fourteen months, and Tanya acts like that's an unnaturally long time for her brother to date someone she hasn't yet met. She says, "But Dale ditched us all when he went off to college halfway across the country, and he never came back."

Dale says nothing. He refills his wine.

I say, "Well, good thing he did, or I wouldn't have met him."

Tanya picks at some bit of food stuck to the face of the utensils drawer. "What is this? Jelly?" Then she asks me if I have any siblings and where do they live?

That one of them lives barely fifty miles away and another just across the state line and Dale hasn't met either also riles up Tanya. "Seriously, is there nobody in your family that you're close to?"

I tell Tanya that I'm close to plenty of people, just not people I share DNA with. When she squints at me, I tell her about my ex-husband, Marco. Married eleven years, divorced three, and we're still friends.

Tanya looks to Dale then. He nods. Actually, Marco is how Dale and I met. They both volunteer as judges in the citywide science fair, elementary division. Every year it's the same projects over and over again, they both say. Which beverage is more harmful to your teeth? How much sunlight do plants really need? Questions that have been answered a million times already. Originality was a tenet in our house when Marco and I were helping Jacob formulate hypotheses for his science fair projects. Internet searches quickly showed us that the human brain can no longer conceive of anything original, but we tried.

Knife in one hand, red beet like the heart of a small mammal in the other, Tanya shakes her head for what feels like five minutes. "Doesn't it make you wonder?" she says finally.

"Wonder what?" I say.

"Well, does everyone else in your family get along well enough?" she says.

Dale's looking out the back window, probably looking for the gray tomcat he's been putting food and water out for. That cat seems to always have some new injury. One time one of its eyes was so swollen, I wanted Dale to take the animal to the vet, but Dale said, "He's feral. How do you expect us to trap him?" Dale calls the cat's injuries "battle scars," says the cat is tough and can take care of himself just fine, which begs the question of why he feeds the animal, but I don't say that because I like that he feeds that cat.

"How would I know?" I say.

"What I'm saying is, if they get along, but you don't, then you're the common denominator, right? Do you ever wonder if maybe it's all on you?"

I know things about Tanya I'm polite enough not to bring up. Mainly that she's been married three times, and that all three husbands were alcoholics who beat her. Common denominators can take many forms, I want to tell her, and I would tell her this, if we were related. And if we were related, she would then tell me that I'm an insensitive asshole. And then I'd say, Excuse me, but who wielded the first criticism here? And then she'd act like she had no idea what I was talking about and she'd go on about how all my life I've been insensitive. And then I'd say, Really? When I was a baby I was insensitive to you? And then she'd say, This is why no one can talk to you. You're always twisting things, always looking for a fight. I'd say, I don't want to fight, but how can we have a relationship if you're allowed to point out my many flaws, but I'm not allowed to say anything about you? Then she'd cry and call up my siblings and tell them what I said to her and then they'd call me one by one to tell me I'm a horrible person.

I look to Dale, who is still looking out the window. A few seconds pass before he notices me watching him, but when he does, he says, "What are you two talking about?" He comes over and rubs the back of my neck with his thumb and forefinger the way that I like. I set down the knife and let my shoulders relax.

High Ground

A mother whose children go to my child's school messaged me and four other mothers from the school because she was in a quandary. Corinne is her name. As most of us knew, Corinne said, she didn't have a good relationship with her sister, who could be controlling and narcissistic.

The truth is, she wrote, she'd been getting along with her sister fairly well these last few months. Then, out of the blue, her sister decided to get angry about something that had happened a year before. Her sister demanded she admit fault and apologize.

Corinne explained that rather than defend herself, she'd decided that for the first time in her life she wasn't going to get into it with her sister. So, she emailed her sister the following note, which she pasted in full: "I'm sorry, but the only kind of relationship I have room for in my life is one that is drama-free. This is not about me and you; it's about Tolliston, the kids, and the new life that will soon be joining our family. When I feel stress, adrenaline courses through my blood, my heart beats faster, and this stresses the baby. Thus, I am not going to talk about this over email or the phone because that never goes well. If you insist on saying something negative to me, then you will need to do it in person at my house, and when Tolliston is present. Perhaps then we can eat and laugh and hug after it's over. Are you still coming over for Easter? We talked about making that bread Mom used to make."

Corinne wrote that we would not believe what her sister did after that. Her sister completely ignored her email, stopped liking anything Corinne posted on Facebook, and then several days later sent each of the kids an Easter card in the mail.

So, here's the quandary, Corinne wrote, should she

A. Throw the Easter cards away? And then feel wasteful and guilty because they're just cards and the kids would love them. Besides, her sister wouldn't know she threw the cards away, so her satisfaction in snubbing her sister would be limited.
B. Write "return to sender" on the cards? And then she risks looking bad for depriving her kids of a relationship with their aunt.
C. Give the kids the cards? She'd be taking the moral high ground, but, on the other hand, her sister would

get what she wants—a relationship with the kids, while being passive-aggressive to Corinne.

No matter what she did, Corinne said, her sister wins; she loses.

The other mothers in the group repeated the same sentiment—that Corinne ought to give the kids the cards. If you can't win no matter what you do, then take the moral high ground, they wrote.

All except Penny, who pointed out that in a battle, one chooses the high ground in order to have the tactical advantage over the opponent they wish to massacre. The idea of choosing the moral high ground is kind of a paradox, she said. There's nothing moral about using the cannon of morality to blow your opponent to bits. Anyway, Penny added, Corinne had already chosen the low ground when she sent that email to her sister. She echoed the consensus that Corinne ought to give the kids the cards, but she stated that doing so would not elevate Corinne to any high ground.

Penny is the same person who last year, when Dana's husband had an affair, asked Dana how she had contributed to the situation their marriage was in. She'd argued that when one partner has an affair, the other partner isn't simply an innocent victim. And that if that person thought of herself or himself as an innocent victim, then it was no wonder that the other partner had had an affair.

After Penny's response, nobody wrote anything else. The message thread disappeared altogether, as though Penny's words had been hand grenades, blitzing every voice.

Except mine. I never responded to Corinne's quandary. Kept my thoughts to myself, reluctant to take a position.

Things My Son Knows

My kid says of our cat, who died this morning, "Maybe he's reincarnated as a fly."

I say, "Why a fly?"

We're settling into his bed to read a bedtime story. Per the usual, the sheets are gritty with the sand he tracks in from the playground at school. I brush the bed off before sitting. I immediately get up again to pull his closet door all the way shut. Not for him, but for me. He asked me once, "Why are you doing that? You afraid there's a monster in there?" "Of course not," I said, "Incomplete things just bother me." "You could open it all the way," he said, "But you never do that." "Then the mess in there would bother me," I said. He seemed skeptical.

He looks at me skeptically now, too. "Do you even know what reincarnation is?"

"Of course, I do," I say.

"Why do you say 'of course'?" he says.

"I've lived a long time. And I read a lot. I know a lot of words. Your mother's pretty knowledgeable."

"Have you been reincarnated?" he asks.

"I don't know. Not that I'm aware of."

"Well, I have," he says. "Thirty-eight times. I've lived longer than you and I'm more knowledgeable than you."

He's sitting up against his bedroom wall, his arms crossed in front of his chest. Serious as a dead cat on a pile of clean laundry. (My favorite pajamas on top. The softest flannel. My kid said, "Well, that *is* a good place to die.")

"Thirty-eight times," I say. "That's a lot of lives. Were you ever a cat?"

He scrunches up his eyes. "Cats aren't reincarnated as people. You can only go the same or smaller."

"How do you know that?" I say.

"I told you. I've been reincarnated 38 times. I know things," he says.

His father, Owen, used to say that every time he surprised me with some bit of trivia I'd never heard him mention before and I asked him how he knew it: "Like I've told you, I know things." Somehow his saying that always made me feel safe, as though with nothing but what he possessed in his head, he could navigate us through any impediment.

"Why?" I ask my son. "Why only the same or smaller?"

My son has often said he wishes he were a cat. So he wouldn't have to go to school. So he wouldn't have to do chores. So he could just eat, play, sleep. I've said, "But consider how little control Ganges has. He has to beg us to feed him." My son said, "That part sounds the same as being a kid."

"I don't know," he says now. "That's just how it is."

Something about his not claiming to know rubs at me. Like Ganges licking, licking, licking the same worn patch of fur. If my son had a rationale, maybe my heart wouldn't feel now like an overcooked slab of steak. Maybe I wouldn't think irrational thoughts, like that breathing in the scent of Ganges in those flannel pajamas might infuse me with Owen.

My idiot brother said maybe it was a blessing my son was too young when Owen died to remember him. I told him to keep his blessings to himself.

My son says now, "You're sad. Are you worried about Ganges being reincarnated as a fly?"

I worry about so many things, ninety percent of which I will not discuss with my son, no matter how articulate and knowledgeable he is.

I say, "A fly is so small and vulnerable."

My son crawls over to me, presents me with his kiss face. Lips so puckered the wet underneath of his lips show, too.

After he kisses me, he says, "You probably feel that way because you kill flies. Treat every fly like it could be Ganges, and you'll feel better."

Barrel Cactus

"You always go for the cactuses," Jennifer says. "There's a lot more to the desert, you know."

I'm digging a hole for my latest purchase—a little barrel cactus plump like Jennifer's toes, the nails of which are painted coal. She's standing over me, shading me from the sun. Ten toes lined up like strange hors d'oeuvres.

I suspect Jennifer's remark is pointed at my mother, who is in the sky right this moment, heading back to Chicago. The entire three days she was here, my mother wouldn't step outside a building or an automobile long enough to really experience the heat, to let it knead her into submission, but that didn't stop her from complaining about it. "How can you stand it here, Sue? Everything's so hostile." Then yesterday evening at the shops downtown my mother bought everything saguaro she could find. Dishes painted with saguaros. Saguaro-shaped soaps and pens. Lollipops for my brother Charlie's kids.

Jennifer was polite. She stocked the fridge with those iced teas my mother likes. She tolerated long hours of my mother talking about church and grandchildren. But while my mother shopped, Jennifer sat out on the curb, closed her eyes, and tilted her face toward the sun. Scratched at the pavement with her fingernails.

When my mother looked out our sliding glass door this morning and said, "Sue, your yard is unwelcoming. How could you possibly have a barbecue out here?" before I could respond, Jennifer said, "What do you care? You don't eat meat."

My mother winced. Retreated to the guest bedroom. Didn't come out until it was time for me to return her to the airport.

Jennifer changed into running clothes, didn't say a word on her way out the door. My mother didn't mention Jennifer's absence when she emerged from the bedroom with that suitcase so huge she could fly home inside it if it weren't so stuffed with souvenirs.

I picked up the barrel cactus on the way back from dropping my mother off.

Jennifer's lived in the desert her whole life. She grew up watching her dad impale rattlesnakes in their backyard with a rake. She didn't care for Chicago when we visited my mother at Thanksgiving. "It's so crowded and so concrete and so cold."

I say now, "I like their armor. Their prickliness makes them beautiful." Like how chainmail is beautiful, and sleek metal helmets that open and close on hinges. When we went to the Art Institute of Chicago during that visit, I spent the entire afternoon in the medieval section.

Jennifer's expression softens. She weaves her way between chunky saguaros and scarlet-studded nopales to retrieve my gloves. Drops them onto the rocks by my knees.

My cactus-planting gloves are some kind of rigid synthetic that can keep out just about any variety of spine. I learned the hard way not to wear leather gloves. Jennifer was the one to explain it to me when I came into the house with a palm full of "sharps"—what she called those spines. She's a pediatric nurse. Holds down little kids and pokes needles into their arms. Scarier than the Tooth Fairy, I say about her at parties, while she rolls her eyes.

"Leather is skin," she said that day I planted my first cactus. "Why would it be any more resistant to being punctured than your own skin?" She tweezed those spines from my gloved hand as casually as she might pluck seeds from a pomegranate.

"I'm going to bartender up something cool and stiff," she says now. "A Horsefeather maybe. We'll get tipsy and we'll hike up to Happy Valley Lookout."

The first time Jennifer suggested a hike in the sun after cocktails, I thought she was shitting me. All anyone ever talks about around here is water and how much of it you lose without knowing it. Because it's a dry heat. You can't feel yourself sweat.

These cactuses are made for this weather, but even they need a good soak from the garden hose once in a while or they shrivel like raisins.

"One more month, and it'll be too hot to hike in the sun," I say, wondering if it's already too hot.

"One more month, and we'd die hiking out there in daylight," Jennifer says. "Especially after a cocktail. Probably today we'll survive, though." She pivots, and I admire the pointy tips of her fibulas, the way they stud her ankles like spurs.

Tea Kettles

I was at the mall to replace a broken tea kettle when I saw one of the dads from my kid's school, the one who's a cop. He looks exactly like what he is. Honest, I call that. The way a good tea kettle looks like a tea kettle, whereas some are designed these days to masquerade as other things—flamingos, giraffes, UFOs. For no good reason at all, other than that people in the world collect such shit. This department store, in fact, sells a tea kettle that resembles a toilet. It doesn't even make sense.

This cop, his name is Donny, keeps his head shaved. His irises look like discs of ice, like if you were to put your finger to his eyeballs, your finger would freeze to them. At a school spaghetti dinner, he showed everyone at our table the raised bump on his bicep where he'd been bitten by a police dog. The word "bump" does not do the scar justice unless you think on the scale of the protuberance and hardness of a baby bump. Or like how a tree oozes out its own liquid bandage when you prune it, only the liquid bandage hardens into an impenetrable barrier. Not that I touched his scar. I mean I'd wanted to, because I'm a curious person. But how would that have looked? Me reaching out to place my hand on Donny's bicep?

Anyway, I spot Donny in the women's lingerie department, staring absent-mindedly at a rack of animal-print bras. Again with the animals.

I think he must be purchasing a gift for his wife, Kate. That woman is on the board of a charity for dogs and is always asking people to attend this or that fundraiser or purchase this or that expensive raffle ticket for makeovers and computer repair certificates and what have you, but then when the middle-school kids are having their bake sales, she's all oh-I-can't-buy-any-of-that-or-I'll-end-up-eating-it-all.

Or maybe since he doesn't seem to be so much considering the animal-print bras as to be resting his focus on them, he's just waiting on Kate while she tries on lingerie. Kate runs with that dog of hers, I know, because I've seen her, and even if I hadn't seen her, I'd know because of those calf muscles. Only runners have calves like that, calves so meaty they make you think of drumsticks, like the way predators in cartoons picture their prey as cuts of meat. What I mean is Kate is probably the type of woman who actually enjoys trying on lingerie.

But the person who comes out of the dressing room isn't Kate but Allison, the mom of that girl in my son's class who he says lives in a shelter. My son, barely seven, told me the girl, Reilly, isn't allowed to see her father or rather he isn't allowed to see her and her mother. Because he threw something at Reilly's mother. Because glass shattered all over the kitchen floor. Because Reilly's mother's cheek turned purple. My son tells me this, and I'm thinking he's too young to know about stuff like this, but then I think about Reilly and all the other kids who know-know stuff like this, and then I just shake my head. My son told me that Reilly both misses her father and doesn't. He said, "I understand that, Mom," and I said, "You do?" "Not about Dad," he said. "Oh," I said. "I mean," he said, "feeling two ways at once. I feel that way a lot, like when I want to go swimming but also I don't because then I have to have a bath after to get the chlorine out, plus the chlorine always makes my penis sting."

I realize I'm not so surprised to see Allison. This Donny guy looks like the kind of guy who would cheat on his wife. Like I said, he looks like what he is.

So, Allison walks out of the dressing room in this summery white dress. It's an eyelet fabric, falls to just below her knees. I think of photographs of Woodstock, only she's a clean, bleached version of that time. And she doesn't have flowers in her hair, though she looks like she could pull that off, like she should be running barefoot through a meadow in that dress. What is it that bear used to say in that laundry detergent (or was it softener?)

commercial? Fresh like a summer's breeze? Something like that. Scratch and sniff Allison, and she'd smell like daisies and fresh-cut grass and pot.

What I've wanted to know ever since my son told me about Reilly and Allison in that shelter is what is her ex like out in the world? Like if he were sitting across from me at a school spaghetti dinner, would he give off a creep vibe? Would I think there's something not right about that guy? Like Donny over there. Not the most charming man I've ever met. Doesn't smile much. Has that steely stare you expect from a cop, particularly if one is pulling you over for speeding. Or was he more like my Carver? Smiling across the table at Donny at that spaghetti dinner. Offering to refill my lemonade. But then later that night, after our son was asleep, he was all everyone-saw-you-staring-at-his-bicep and don't-you-fucking-embarrass-me-like-that-again. Carver is like a tea kettle disguised as a sheep.

Migration

For our ten-year anniversary, Ben surprises me with a sheep festival in Idaho. The crowning event is the herding of the sheep through the center of this little town, migrating from a depleted pasture to a lush pasture. "So many sheep you can't walk," Ben said when he told me about the trip. We looked at photos of onlookers penned in against storefronts, the street blanketed in wooly white.

We haven't experienced the herding yet ourselves because it's only Tuesday, the day of soap-making and sausage-eating and fucking between lunch and dinner. That's our itinerary, Ben tells me after spitting a mouthful of mint into the hotel sink.

These days, fucking between lunch and dinner is as out of the ordinary as soap-making. Fucking at any hour is out of the ordinary at this stage of our marriage. But our four-year-old is with Ben's parents for the week, and we're far, far away from our dirty house with its smelly laundry and crusty dishes and sticky floors. So, if we don't fuck on this trip, then that means we have a more serious problem than the temporary problem of being exhausted parents of a four-year-old.

This is a lot of pressure.

It's akin, I tell Ben, to going out to dinner on Valentine's Day. Sitting before a plate of oysters, a single red rose in a vase between us, surrounded by so many other hetero couples sitting before plates of oysters, single red roses in vases on their tables, too, I feel as sexy as a sheep traveling in a herd to greener pasture.

"Would you rather we don't have time alone?" Ben whispers in the soap shop.

He passes me bottle after bottle of essential oils. I sniff and shake my head at every one.

"That's not what I mean," I say. "I just wish we could have normal, no-pressure time alone, like sitting on the sofa with our feet up, eating leftover take-out Thai for dinner. Like we used to."

"I thought you liked traveling. I thought you liked trying new things," he says. He's been really excited about this trip. Proud of himself for taking initiative, proud for coming up with a novel idea that would pass my anti-herding-mentality sniff test. His brother, Craig, and Craig's wife, Lottie, are always going on cruises or to plasticky beach resorts for their vacations, and Ben, who wouldn't mind a week at a beach resort himself, knows me well enough to know he's not going to get a moan out of me at a beach resort.

"I do," I say. "But when it comes to sex—"

Here, Ben puts his finger to his lips, tells me to lower my voice.

"The problem is we don't have a baseline," I say.

"We have a baseline. It's just zero," Ben says. Eucalyptus oil in hand, he heads to the colors station. He doesn't look at me. He focuses hard on the colored soaps, trying to look like he actually cares a lot about the color of soap.

"Not zero," I say, slipping my hand into Ben's back pocket. "Maybe twelve on a scale of a hundred?"

He smiles in spite of himself, and we have a good time after that. We stir warm sheep's milk with lye and eucalyptus and the green dye Ben picks out. We pour our mixture into molds. Because the soap takes a day to set, we leave it behind while we eat sausage and drink red wine from clear plastic cups.

"You know just how to seduce me," I say between bites of sausage-on-a-stick doused in hot mustard. Ben reaches under the table and rubs my thigh.

After a bottle and a half of red wine in plastic cups, we stumble hand-in-hand through the town back to our B&B.

As we circle past the main house to our cottage, I see the caretakers through the large kitchen window. He is standing by the screened door smoking a cigarette. She is drying a blue bowl with a dingy dishcloth. She looks so tired. She told me earlier when we arrived that between three kids and the B&B, she barely has time to wash her hair, and I thought to myself, her hair does look a little dirty.

She made time to bake us tiny currant scones sprinkled in powdered sugar, though. She made time to assemble a platter of grapes and cheeses and crackers. We find these sitting on the dining table of our cottage when we open the door. In the fridge is a dainty pitcher of lavender lemonade.

When Ben puts his mouth on mine and backs me into the bed covered in a pretty pale blue quilt, I can't stop picturing that tired woman in the window drying that bowl. I picture her stirring the scone batter in that bowl. Picture her slicing thin slivers of cheese, washing the grapes. I don't tell Ben this, though. He's worked so hard to get me here. The woman in that window has worked hard to get me here, too. I shut my eyes, and I moan.

Manhandle

I'm taking a bath with my kid, and he points and says, "What's that?"

"My vagina," I say, thinking he's forgotten the word again. I can't tell you how many times he's referred to my "penis" and I've had to correct him.

"No, that hair," he says.

"It's hair," I say.

"I mean why do you have hair there?" he says, making a face.

"I don't know, but it's normal," I say.

"Why don't you shave it off? It's gross," he says.

"That's mean," I say. I see why pubic hair seems strange to him, though, out of place. Like finding an ear behind your knee, I suppose. Mine is probably the only body he's seen naked besides his own. My husband/his father, Nash, has never ever taken a bath with our son.

"Your dad has hair there, too. You haven't seen it?" I say.

"No," he says.

"Well, he does. He has hair all over his chest and arms and legs as well. And you probably will, too, someday."

My son has selective hearing. Doesn't respond to my forecast, just as he won't respond to my telling him over and over again to put on his pajamas, but mention hot chocolate with whipped cream, and he comes running. He says now, "You shave your legs. Why not shave this hair, too? It's so ugly I can't look at it." But he doesn't cover his eyes.

Sometimes, though not today, he asks if he can have a drink from my "milk bags," even though I stopped nursing him when he was two. Every time, I tell him there is no more milk, that he drank it all. Every time I correct him: breasts, not bags.

What Nash says when I tell him about this conversation: "When are you going to stop taking baths with him? When he's fifteen?"

"Six is still plenty young," I say. "Besides, why shouldn't he know about adult bodies? Maybe this is a good opportunity to teach him to be respectful?" I say this, even though lately I've also been thinking it may be time to stop taking baths with our son. Because I'm getting sick of the assessments, sick of the disregard for the names for things.

I'm sick, too, sometimes of how my son grabs at my body as though it belongs to him. When I'm cooking dinner, he tries to climb me like I'm a ladder. When I'm trying to read, he throws himself on top of me. Puts his hands over my eyes. "Stop manhandling me," I say, and Nash, if he's around to hear, says, "You and your words. He's a child." Then I say, "Manhandle: to handle roughly."

Nash doesn't like the word *menstruation*, either. Doesn't like how openly I talk to our son about it. He used to respond to menstruation talk with the same angry shushing he gives me every time I let slip a *shit* or a *motherfucker*. I gave him hell about that, though. "Why shouldn't he know about menstruation? Why shouldn't he grow up to be informed and sensitive to the women in his life?" Nash didn't say a word about it again, though sometimes he groans a little under his breath when I say I can't take our son to that birthday party or this baseball practice because it's my heaviest day and I'm losing so much blood it's a wonder I'm not dead.

I say to Nash, "If he saw you naked once in a while, he wouldn't think pubic hair was just some monstrosity of his mother's body."

Nash says, "What do you want me to do? Say, 'Son, I'm going to take my clothes off now so you can look at my naked body?'"

"Well, you don't have to be so creepy about it," I say.

"I don't know how not to be creepy about it. That's the thing. There's no natural time for him to see me naked."

It's not just that I sometimes take baths with our son. He's constantly wandering into the bathroom when I'm showering or using the toilet or getting dressed. How Nash has managed to be naked in our house for some brief period every day of our son's life without being seen by our son, I can't understand. It's a mystery on par with the construction of the Egyptian pyramids or with how some people talk aloud in movie theaters, not even trying to keep their voices low. Just yesterday, I was at the movie theater, having left work early after a terrible meeting during which a male coworker cut me off mid-sentence no fewer than three times, and this guy two seats away kept asking the woman next to him questions about what was happening in the movie. *Why is she doing that? What do you think that's supposed to mean?* Then when the credits began, he pronounced the movie the dumbest movie he'd ever seen in his life. He said those words with such disdain and righteousness I wanted to slap him. I wanted to say, Where's your movie, asshole? What have you ever done? What have you ever made?

Muscle Memory

The first time Thea met her husband's extended family, his eighty-one-year-old grandfather waggled his tongue at her. He asked if she was single. Thea's husband, Roland, said, "He's got dementia. He doesn't know what he's saying."

Roland was always making excuses for men. The guy who cut Thea in line at the post office: he probably just didn't see her. The guy who honked at her while she was running, startling her so that she tripped and scraped her palms and her chin on the cement: he was probably just trying to compliment her.

Thea said, "Am I supposed to feel better knowing that if he had his wits about him, he'd merely be thinking about waggling his tongue at me?"

Roland groaned.

*

The one man Roland didn't make excuses for was his brother, Trey. He had plenty to say about Trey. That past week, for example, in the kitchen of the beach house Thea's mother-in-law rented for a family vacation because she'd lamented how the eight of them never got together: Roland wanted to know what in hell happened to the leftover meat pie from the night before. Trey said, "When the muscles are hungry, you got to feed them," which prompted Roland to say, "Which muscle was hungry exactly? Your stomach? Your tongue?" Trey, squeezing a fleshy-pink stress ball so that it bulged in and out from the gap between his thumb and forefinger, said, "Well, for its mass, the tongue does use up more calories than any other muscle. I guess that makes it one of the strongest muscles in the body."

Roland: "Where'd you read that?"

Trey: "Somewhere."

Roland: "First, what muscle is the strongest depends on the body. Second, it depends on how you're measuring strength. Third, no."

Trey: "The tongue's the strongest."

Roland: "Even the jaw is stronger than the tongue."

Trey: "I thought you said it depends on the body."

Later that morning, on the beach, Thea and Roland were running off the previous evening's dinner, the meat pies, and Roland said, "He calls meat pies clean eating? Those meat pies are downright dirty."

Thea: "Those meat pies are slutty. He might have a point about the tongue, though. I bet my tongue is stronger than my jaw."

Roland: "Not a chance."

Thea: "Think about it: my tongue has managed to push my teeth with such force I can't even bite through a banana on the left side of my mouth."

Roland: "Before you got a night guard, you grinded so hard with the teeth that do come together, you practically filed them flat. Score a point for the jaw."

Thea: "But you have to admit I have a strong tongue."

*

Eleven years after the tongue waggling incident, Thea could picture her husband's grandfather only one way—hunched in a metal chair, ball cap on his head, dull pink tongue poking out of his mouth like a fat slug.

At the beach rental house, Trey's wife, Arlene, showed Thea photos of their kids hugging their great-grandfather at the nursing home, and Thea cringed.

When they played Apples to Apples Junior with their niece and nephew, and the adjective was "Brave" and Roland laid down a noun card that read, "My Grandfather," Thea, the judge of that round, chose six-year-old Marissa's card, "Jell-O." Roland said, "Jell-O? Brave?!" Thea said, "I happen to have a lot of respect for Jell-O." Roland said nothing more, but Thea knew what he was thinking. Roland often said her #1 fault was she didn't let things go. "Release," he said to her sometimes, as though commanding a dog to drop a stick.

*

After thirteen years together, Thea still had to remind Roland sometimes that she didn't like it when he squeezed her breasts as though he were wringing a wet towel.

Also, every time they flew and he had that damn backpack on, he forgot that the space he occupied extended beyond his physical back. He whacked bystanders in the shoulders or the chest, and, at least once, the face.

*

When they returned from the beach house trip, Thea's dentist had moved to Seattle. Her new dentist freaked out about her open bite when she opened her mouth, said he'd never seen anything like it. He warned about the risk of TMJ and of the teeth that do come together wearing away as a result of the strain. He referred her to an orthodontic surgeon. The orthodontic surgeon said he could break her jaw and graft in bone from her hip to make the teeth on the left side of her mouth come together. But unless she retrained her tongue, it would push her teeth apart again. And at her age, it was far too late to retrain her tongue.

Acknowledgments

I'm so grateful to all my readers, of early drafts and published drafts alike, as well as to the friends and family who have championed my work. Most especially, thank you to my first and always reader, Kim Magowan, whose opinion I value so much, who makes my writing better.

Thanks to Meagan Cass for believing in this book enough to choose it as winner of the Katherine Anne Porter Prize in Short Fiction and to the good people at UNT Press for publishing it.

I'm grateful to my partner, Chris, whose willingness to take on many mundane and thankless tasks helps ensure I have time to write. I'm grateful to my son, Atticus, for his stories and for sharing them with me. And my honorary family, Brandi, who has been one of my biggest supporters from the start.

Finally, thank you to the editors of the journals and anthologies where these stories were originally published, sometimes in slightly different form:

"Accomplice or Hostage" in *Jellyfish Review*

"Killer Tomatoes" in *Corium Magazine*

"How I Learned About Evolution" in *Okay Donkey*

"Men Decide They Want Something" in *Hobart*

"Knife Rules" in *Coffin Bell Journal*

"Parts We Can Live Without" in *Arroyo Literary Review*

"A Treatise on the Broken Heart Idiom" in *Spelk*

"Fish Story" in *New World Writing*

"Lessons" in *Cleaver Magazine*

"Cubist Mother" in *100 Word Story* (and reprinted in *Tell It Slant: Creating, Refining, and Publishing Creative Nonfiction*, 3rd edition)

"Dendrochronology" in *Scoundrel Time* (and reprinted in *Flash Flood*)

"Bargain" in *Litro*

"Sockets" in *Gone Lawn*

"A Girl Scout is Useful, Thrifty, Cheerful, Courteous, Clean in Thought, and Above All, Loyal" in *DIAGRAM*

"Hostages" in *Ghost Parachute* (and reprinted in *Ghost Parachute: 105 Flash Fiction Stories*)

"Hail Satan" in *Hermeneutic Chaos*

"Before After" in *Spelk*

"Why Science Lessons That Involve Potatoes Give Me Grief" in *Threadcount*

"Dollhouse Furniture" in *The Nottingham Review*
"Phainopepla" in *Cease, Cows*
"Fertilizer" in *Pithead Chapel* (and reprinted in *Best Microfiction 2020*)
"Three Ways to Eat Quince" in *Word Riot*
"An Arm or a Palm Frond or a Boot" in *Pidgeonholes*
"What We Expect to See" in *Paper Darts*
"Feng Shui" in *Bodega*
"Glow" in *Arroyo Literary Review*
"The Funny Thing" in *Nashville Review*
"The Scream Queen Is Bored" in *Angels Flight · literary west*
"Tobe's Baby" in *Jellyfish Review*
"I'm Just Talking About Water" in *Occulum*
"The Point" in *Longleaf Review*
"Impulses" in *Tiny Molecules*
"Before and After" in *Fanzine*
"Palate Cleanser" in *Bending Genres* (and reprinted in *Best Microfiction 2020* and the *Bending Genres Anthology: 2018/2019*)
"Eden" in *MoonPark Review*
"Binary Code" in *Monkeybicycle*
"One or Two?" in *Passages North*
"Business Enough" in *Knee-Jerk*
"Snapshot" in *Atlas and Alice*

"Deposition" in *Milk Candy Review*

"Night Bloom" in *The Forge*

"Dead Plant" in *FRiGG*

"Carrot" in *formercactus*

"Snow White with Goats" in *Wigleaf*

"Cake or Pie" in *Wigleaf* (and reprinted in *Best Small Fictions 2021*)

"Frogs in Captivity" in *Spelk*

"My Husband Is Always Losing Things" in *Cleaver Magazine*

"Return" in *New South*

"No Knees" in *The Journal of Compressed Creative Arts*

"Common Denominator" in *FRiGG*

"High Ground" in *New World Writing*

"Things My Son Knows" in *jmww*

"Barrel Cactus" in *FRiGG*

"Tea Kettles" in *Okay Donkey*

"Migration" in *Fictive Dream*

"Manhandle" in *Jellyfish Review*

"Muscle Memory" in *Hobart*